DRIVE-THRU OF THE DEAD

DRAYTON FALLS VOLUME 1

BRYAN SMITH

TABLE OF CONTENTS

This one is for my "buy a character name" patrons.

Christopher Schaefer
Christina Pfeiffer
Bridgett Nelson

Thank you for your support.

DRIVE-THRU OF THE DEAD

ONCE UPON A TIME IN a shitty little southern town called Drayton Falls, a lot of fucked up shit happened. I phrase it that way because that's how so many old-timey stories begin, but in truth the fucked up shit to which I refer has never been confined to a single brief or definable period. A lot of folks in these parts will tell you, in all seriousness, that Drayton Falls is cursed, and there are more stories purporting to explain the origins of the curse than there are stars in the sky. Some say the soil itself is tainted in some way, perhaps by all the innocent native blood spilled on it by settlers centuries ago.

Whatever the truth is, one thing is indisputable, and that's something is rotten in Drayton Falls. The entire history of the place is rife with tales of the weird and unexplainable, as well as the just plain fucked up as all get-out. At one point, way back in the not-so-golden-olden days, things got so bad people took to calling it Drayton's Folly, a monicker that for a while became so prevalent it even got printed on a number of semi-official maps around the turn of the twentieth century.

Perhaps the most interesting thing about the town is how, despite its less than shining reputation, it has not only persisted in existing but actually thrives in a strange kind of half-assed way. You'd expect a bad luck burg like the one I've described to become a ghost town at some point, but the population as of the last census was just a shade under 20,000. Located in a valley smack in the middle of nowhere, it's the biggest little town out there in the wide gulf between the big cities in this state. A lot of the town's citizens grow up hating it, but not many of them leave, at least not for good. People get stuck in small-town life, for better or worse, unable to imagine making it in the big, bad city.

I've lived in Drayton Falls all my life.

I know all its sordid stories and deep, dark secrets.

And this is one of them.

~

Dave Shepherd was new to working the graveyard shift at Big Fiesta Burgers. He'd had no prior experience in the fast-food industry, unless being a frequent customer counted, but he figured it'd be easy and the biggest challenge he'd face would be dealing with stoner customers who got confused by the presence of "Fiesta" in the restaurant's name and wanted to order tacos and burritos at 2:45 in the morning.

At no point prior to starting his first shift had he expected he'd spend so much of his time on the clock dealing with the living dead.

But we're getting ahead of ourselves here.

We'll get back to the reanimated dead folks soon enough, but first you're gonna need to know a little more about our friend Dave.

Manning a late-night drive-thru wasn't the type of work Dave had envisioned as a career when he was younger. As a boy, he'd harbored the typical big dreams of being rich and famous some way or other, fantasies that for him most often centered around somehow becoming either a Hollywood action star or a homerun-hitting major league baseball player. For Dave, accomplishing these dreams was tragically compromised by a little thing called "reality".

He possessed no thespian skills and wasn't nearly good-looking enough to star in his cousin Billy's backyard amateur camcorder movies, never mind headlining some million-dollar Hollywood special effects extravaganza. As for baseball, he'd never played the game in any type of organized league, not even Pee Wee, which as it turned out was a significant hindrance to his aspirations of becoming the next Babe Ruth. The time he tried out for the high school team without having previously played anything other than underhand pitch streetball would likely forever remain one of the most humiliating moments of his life. He was jeered off the field within minutes. Some of the real players threw things at him, hastening his tearful departure. Rocks, clumps of dirt, soda cans, nine-volt batteries, small kittens ... whatever they could find.

This event so emotionally devastated him he quit school rather than face the embarrassment of being subjected to the same ridicule every subsequent day until graduation. His parents were disappointed but not surprised. He begged them to move to another town so he could start over, but they told him they didn't believe in his future enough to make the effort. His father told his poker buddies it'd be like investing in a company that'd already gone tits up. Dave was in the room when the old man said this. The way all those beer-bellied old assholes had laughed and laughed hadn't been quite as humiliating as his baseball failure, not even when they made fun of him for crying, but it was a close thing.

His mom told him he needed to "toughen up" and advised joining the army. Dave gave it some thought. For about twenty minutes. He imagined being screamed at by a hard-as-nails drill sergeant like that dude in *Full Metal Jacket* and realized he just wasn't cut out for serving his country.

Instead he applied for a job at a car wash, and when he was hired the next day, he felt a thrill of accomplishment for one of the few times in his life. He beamed with pride as he announced the news to his parents, who both made fun of him for acting like he'd just gotten into Harvard or hired on with Microsoft.

By then he knew it was pointless to seek their approval for anything he did. He moved out and rented a room above the garage of the car wash owner's house, a roach-infested space that wasn't connected to the central HVAC. It was too cold in winter and sweltering in summer. Nonetheless, he lived there for two and a half years ... until the car wash went out of business, sending Dave into a mad scramble for new gainful employment.

At first he had no luck at all in this pursuit. He filled in dozens of job applications all around town. Weeks passed, then months. His meager savings from the car wash job ran out, resulting in his eviction from the gross garage apartment. His parents again exhibited nothing but scorn and laughter when he begged to move back in. What made this extra galling was the surprise return of his older brother to the old homestead.

Dave had last seen Gary Shepherd right before he was sent off to prison for mutilating cattle and then fornicating with the remains while under the influence of Belgian toad venom, which was tons more potent than ordinary toad venom. Dave hadn't even known Gary was getting paroled. He was just there when he showed up, hanging out on the back patio with a live chicken held in his lap in a way that struck Dave as troublesome given Gary's sordid history with farm animals. Gary wasn't even gainfully employed yet and their parents were letting him stay with them. They just felt so sorry for their oldest and believed he needed time and space to heal from the trauma of incarceration.

The family didn't need another leech.

Dave was told to take a hike.

His dad and brother threw beer cans at him as he made his sullen way down the driveway to his 1977 Ford Pinto, which now doubled as his new home. Just as things looked their bleakest—and as he was contemplating a possible career as probably the world's least popular male prostitute—Dave walked into Big Fiesta Burgers and was hired on the spot by Randall "Hacksaw" Farnsworth, the manager of the franchise. No one he spoke to admitted to knowing why he was called Hacksaw and other employees advised Dave not to ask.

He was told he could start that night. They needed someone on the overnight shift because most of the staff had quit the night before. Another, less desperate person might have thought twice before accepting a position at a joint where the turnover rate was higher than that of the death row at a Texas penitentiary, but by that point Dave's funds were down to the handful of change in his pocket. He couldn't even afford a quart of beer without bankrupting himself.

He was three hours into his first shift when he had his first truly strange interaction with a customer. Up to that point, working the drive-thru had been a way more chill experience than he'd expected. His one good friend in life was a guy named Fat Bob who'd been the cashier at the car wash. Fat Bob had once upon a time been a drive-thru attendant at a McDonald's. According to Fat Bob, it'd been hell on earth, the pace so hectic and the customers so mean he ended up having an epic breakdown that put him in a mental hospital for over a year. Dave suspected there was more to that story than Fat Bob let on, but he figured the man's cautionary words about working in the fast-food industry could be trusted.

Big Fiesta Burgers was a whole other world from McDonald's, though. By the time he hit that three-hour mark of his first shift, Dave was convinced he must be working for the world's least popular restaurant. He'd taken three orders, two of which he got wrong because he hit the wrong keys on the computer. Even in the dead of night, one customer per hour struck him as a pretty sorry average. He couldn't fathom why they even bothered keeping a drive-thru open overnight.

A beep sounded in his ear, alerting him to the arrival of the fourth customer of his shift. "Hey, welcome to Big ..." He trailed off for a moment, momentarily forgetting where he worked. Then it came to him and he continued. "Sorry, technical issues. Welcome to Big Kahuna Burgers. How can I help you?"

He frowned, belatedly recognizing what he'd said wasn't what he'd meant to say.

Then it came to him.

Big Kahuna Burgers? What the fuck is wrong with you, Dave? This ain't Pulp *fuckin'* Fiction*!*

He considered correcting himself but decided there was no point in drawing attention to the error. From what he knew of the restaurant's typical clientele, chances were good the mistaken utterance had gone unnoticed anyway. A great many of them were probably too high to correctly identify which restaurant they'd pulled into without driving around to the front to see the big light-up sign.

The hiss coming through the earpiece of his headset indicated he still had an open circuit, but whoever had pulled up to the speaker wasn't saying anything.

Not knowing what else to do, he repeated the greeting.

"Welcome to Big Kahuna Burgers ..."

Goddammit.

A chuckle from somewhere nearby made him glance over at Kelsey Robbins, the only other employee on duty. Kelsey was a rail-thin girl who was about five feet tall and had hair that was a dirty shade of blonde. Like nearly everyone else he'd ever known, she'd started dishing out the insulting remarks about his looks and intelligence almost from the get-go. All night long she'd been asking him about his lobotomy. Did it still hurt or make him sad to think about? Did he have a metal plate in his head and if so was he able to pick up radio station signals in his brain? Did his parents tie strings of raw meat around his neck just to get dogs to play with him when he was a child?

After about a full hour of unrelenting abuse, he gave up trying to tell her he'd never had a lobotomy and that dogs liked him just fine. This time he flipped her off without looking and repeated the greeting again, finally getting it right on the third try.

Still no reply.

He turned and looked at the black-and-white monitor mounted on the wall behind him. An old Honda hatchback sat idling near the speaker pole. The image was fuzzy because all the tech at Big Fiesta Burgers was old and purchased secondhand from joints that'd gone out of business ages ago. He could tell there were two people sitting in the front of the car, but he couldn't make out much about their faces. They were just sitting there, the driver staring straight ahead instead of leaning out the window or even looking at the speaker pole.

"Tell them to pull up to the window."

That was Kelsey.

She was right next to him, so close their bodies were nearly touching. Dave felt his cheeks grow hot from the physical proximity. He cringed in anticipation of another round of insults, but she appeared not to have noticed his nervous reaction.

She was looking at the monitor, a strange expression on her face.

Dave touched the mute button on his headset. "Is something wrong?"

She stared at the screen a moment longer, saying nothing.

Then she shook her head. "Just tell them to pull up, fuck-knuckle. I'll be right back."

She moved away from him, disappearing down a hallway. He knew she'd opened the heavy door to the supply room by the creaking sound that followed seconds later. Other noises ensued. Boxes being shoved aside. Something made of glass shattering as it fell off a high shelf and hit the floor.

What the hell was she doing back there?

Dave looked at the monitor.

Nothing had changed.

He unmuted the headset and said, "Please pull up to the window."

The Honda hatchback stayed where it was a moment longer before it at last began to roll forward, moving out of range of the camera out back. Dave observed through the window as the car came around the side of the building. A sense of deep apprehension came over him even before the hatchback drifted to a slow stop alongside the window, which he'd left open, a choice he now believed fell firmly into the category of Colossal Fucking Mistakes I Will Soon Regret. Something was really off about the dudes in this car, possibly in a dangerous way. This was the middle of the night in a lonely area with hardly anyone around. It was just occurring to him how often people who worked late-night jobs in places like this or at gas stations got held up at gunpoint.

Sometimes even got shot. Or killed.

He was reaching to press the button that would close the window when he noticed the guy behind the steering wheel of the hatchback staring at him. With considerable reluctance, Dave met the guy's disconcerting, unblinking gaze. His mouth opened to regurgitate the proper greeting yet again, but this time the words never made it past his lips.

The color of the man's skin was an unhealthy-looking faded gray. His lank hair was a dingy corn-yellow. He looked thin to the point of starvation, his features gaunt, almost skeletal beneath the papery skin. His mouth opened, emitting a groaning exhalation of sour breath. The groaning went on and on. His eyes had a rotten, milky look, dotted with points of red. His clothes were filthy, as if he'd been rolling around in dirt.

Dave shuddered. "Dude ... you look like shit. Like, I think you might be fucking dying or something. For real. What I'm saying is I think you need a doctor more than you need one of our shitty burgers."

The man's only reply was more of that spooky groaning. His passenger seat companion was making the same sound. Together they formed a chorus of inarticulate noise. The noise got steadily louder, becoming infused with a note of vague agitation.

Dave shook his head. "I don't know what you motherfuckers are trying to tell me. Are you here to file a complaint? Did you have some kind of fucked up reaction to our food?"

The driver's mouth twitched.

He made a new sound, one that might have been the softest of chuckles.

Heh ... heh ... heh.

Or maybe that was just Dave's imagination.

Then the driver leaned out of the Honda's window, raising out of his seat as he reached out with the apparent intention of pulling himself through the open drive-thru window. Rather than immediately hitting the button to close the window, Dave recoiled in fright, taking two quick steps backward. He was on the verge of calling out to Kelsey for help when the driver was forced to slither back behind the wheel of the Honda. The car had started rolling forward again

7

because he'd taken his foot off the brake without first moving the shifter over to park.

Dave heaved a huge sigh of relief.

A relief that was short-lived.

Because there was no line of impatient customers idling behind the Honda, the driver was able to shift gears again and back up. How a person in such rough shape could operate a vehicle at all baffled Dave. It was a situation that stood in defiance of all things logical and reasonable. The guy looked *frail*, like a barely held-together collection of desiccated body parts and stringy sinew. He looked like he belonged in a drawer at the morgue rather than behind the wheel of an automobile.

The driver worked the shifter again, groaning in louder agitation as he grappled with it, wrenching it this way and that in an increasingly desperate effort to set the brake. The effort attained a level of such stupefying clumsiness Dave found it strangely compelling. It was like watching a caveman attempting to bludgeon his way through basic car stuff. At one point he considered giving the poor bastard some pointers, then thought better of it, remembering what he really wanted was for these weird assholes to move along. On top of all that, it was extra weird how the guy had managed to back the car up with no problem whatsoever but now, just a few seconds later, was having so much difficulty. Dave had an idea this dude didn't have a whole lot of fully functioning brain cells to start with and what few he had left were shutting down.

At last, through sheer dumb luck more than anything else, the driver managed to pop the shifter into the right slot.

Then he looked at Dave again.

And began making a second attempt to crawl out of the car and through the drive-thru window.

Which was still open.

Fuck a goddamn duck.

Dave again reached for the button to close the window.

That was when he heard Kelsey again, finally emerged from the back room, standing right behind him now. "Move, motherfucker."

He glanced back at her and his eyes went wide when he saw the pump shotgun gripped in her hands.

"Um ..."

Sighing, she shoved him out of the way and stepped forward just in time to press the muzzle of the shotgun's barrel against the groaning man's forehead.

Dave figured the big gun was for show more than anything else, a last resort tool of intimidation Big Fiesta Burgers employees could use to make troublesome late-night customers behave. He knew for a fact having the muzzle of that long barrel pressed against his own head would chill him out in a hurry in the unlikely event he ever tried anything as braindead as what this guy was doing.

It probably wasn't even loaded.

Kelsey squeezed the trigger and the shotgun boomed, a sound so huge it caused Dave to jump three feet straight backward. He felt like his skeleton had tried launching itself right out of his body. The top of the groaning man's head blew apart like an overripe melon, throwing blood, brain tissue, and splintered bone shards all over the drive-thru station.

It was a hell of a mess.

The man was no longer groaning for the simple reason that he was dead, those last few remaining brain cells blasted into oblivion. His body was hanging half in and half out of the restaurant, having collapsed at an angle affording Dave an unimpeded view of the cratered remaining lower half of his head, which resembled an oozing pile of bloody jelly.

Shotgun still clutched in her hands, Kelsey stepped out from behind the counter and went to the locked door at the side of the restaurant. Shifting to a one-handed grip on the gun, she unlocked the door with a key attached to a retractable zip cord she kept clipped to her belt.

As she shouldered the door open, she glanced back at Dave, sneering as she said, "Come on, motherfucker. I can't do this on my own."

Her tone indicated she expected immediate compliance and under ordinary circumstances he'd be inclined to do whatever she told him. Though their job titles were the same, she was effectively his boss on the two-person shift, having more than a year of seniority on him. She knew all the ins and outs of working in fast food while he was a day-one newbie still winging it. Despite the verbal abuse she hurled at him, deferring to her in virtually all matters was a no-brainer.

His gaze flicked briefly back to the guy she'd just blown away.

Speaking of no-brainers ...

"*Dave!*"

Hearing his name shouted at high volume made him jump

backward again, almost like a startled cat, in that he felt right on the verge of turning tail and running out of the room. He gaped at Kelsey, his throat working as his brain scrambled for words it couldn't quite find. A response was required, he knew that, but his brain was short-circuiting.

Kelsey screeched in frustration. "Am I gonna have to come over there and kick you square in the nuts? Because you better believe I will if you don't get your ass in gear."

Dave believed her.

He swallowed a lump in his throat that felt approximately the size of a grapefruit. "Okay. Shit. I'm coming. Chill out."

Stepping out from behind the counter, he followed her out of the restaurant, where they stood for a moment on the sidewalk as Kelsey glanced out at the empty street. Big Fiesta Burgers was located on a lightly traveled secondary road on the dreary outskirts of Drayton Falls, where the bulk of its customer base derived from a decaying nearby housing development built in the sixties and a trailer park a couple miles down the road. Even during its busiest hours, the restaurant did only a tiny fraction of the business of the big chain places.

Dave got the feeling she was worried someone else with a terminal case of the late-night munchies might come along and complicate whatever it was she meant to do next. The odds of this happening within at least the next little while seemed relatively low given how slow it'd been all night, but he supposed you never knew when some drunk from the trailer park, frustrated by bare cupboards and an empty fridge in the midst of a binge, might decide to venture out and visit Big Fiesta in the middle of the night.

Dave cleared his throat. "Can I ask you something?"

Kelsey's gaze stayed on the empty street. "That depends."

"On what?"

She grunted. "How fucking stupid it is."

He stuffed his hands in his pockets and scuffed his shoe at the sidewalk, frowning as his gaze tracked a discarded food wrapper blowing across the nearly empty parking lot. "Hmm."

Kelsey made a sound of exasperation. "Fuck. Just say it, whatever it is."

Dave looked at her, a look of keen, earnest interest on his face. "Why is it called Big *Fiesta* Burgers? In perusing the menu, I see only standard American burger joint fare and nothing incorporating even a vague Mexican flavor. We don't even offer jalapenos as an optional topping."

Kelsey closed her eyes and groaned. "Oh my fucking god."

Dave frowned. "What?"

She opened her eyes and looked at him. "We've got serious business to tend to and you're asking me about the incongruous nature of our fucking *menu?*"

Far from the first time, Dave winced at her harsh, belligerent tone. "I was just curious. Also, I guess I was kind of avoiding the elephant in the room, by which I mean the way you straight up murdered that drunk dude."

She rolled her eyes. "I didn't *murder* anybody, motherfucker. Also, he wasn't drunk."

Dave tilted his head, giving her a dubious look. "I'm sorry, but what makes you say that? The guy seemed pretty drunk to me, and unless I hallucinated you blowing his brains out all over the drive-thru station, then yeah, Kelsey, you murdered the poor bastard. I mean, I'm no snitch. Ask anybody. If covering it up is what we're doing here, cool, whatever. Just, you know ... I saw what I saw."

Kelsey sighed. "Again, Dave, I didn't *murder* anybody."

Dave's face twisted in deepening confusion. "Hmm. Well, look—"

Before he could press the issue further, sounds from the direction of the parked Honda drew their eyes that way. The dead groaning guy's passenger seat companion, who'd remained where he was until just a moment ago, was now attempting to crawl out the open window on his side. He was going about it as clumsily as his deceased friend had operated the vehicle, hanging out of the window and reaching toward the ground with lazily grasping hands.

Kelsey stepped off the sidewalk and approached him, raising the shotgun again as she drew near.

Dave hurried after her. "Whoa, hold up, don't do—"

She placed the muzzle of the shotgun against the back of the man's skull and squeezed the trigger. The close-range report of the shotgun was just as startling as it'd been the first time. Blood and brains splashed against dirty asphalt from a gaping forehead exit wound. Stunned to have witnessed a second act of shocking, deadly violence, Dave's reaction was similar to the previous time, a cat-like backward jump that left him feeling like his skeleton had tried escaping his body. The casual, almost offhanded way his coworker had killed two men defied comprehension, as if she were some kind of ice-in-her-veins gangland executioner.

As best he could tell, the only sin the dead men had committed was pulling up to the wrong fast-food joint at the wrong fucking time. The thing of trying to crawl in through the drive-thru window was a mild annoyance at best. The man hadn't even been armed. Surely it would've been preferable to deal with the situation by some non-lethal means, but instead here he was, an involuntary accessory to slaughter.

Kelsey glanced back at him. "What's wrong with you?"

Dave spent a moment tittering like a deranged little ghost girl in a horror movie. The absurdity of Kelsey's question in juxtaposition with what he'd witnessed made him feel like he was losing his mind. Maybe he really was hallucinating every bit of this weird night. Maybe Kelsey had dosed his soda with some funky psychoactive drug. He might have gone on giggling in the same borderline unhinged manner a while longer if not for what happened next.

Kelsey pointed the shotgun at him. "Knock that shit off right the fuck now."

Dave knocked that shit off.

He now had definitive proof of how immediately sobering it could be to have the large muzzle of a powerful firearm aimed straight at his chest. He stopped giggling and his semi-deranged smile evaporated. "I'm sorry. I say that in all deep sincerity, despite not being sure why I'm apologizing to the homicidal crazy lady with a shotgun. I suppose you're about to tell me you didn't just murder your second motherfucker of the night."

She nodded. "That's right. I haven't murdered anybody tonight."

Kelsey was no longer aiming the shotgun at him, but Dave's wariness of it remained.

"Look, I'm not trying to be difficult, but please make this make sense. You're telling me my eyes are lying. I didn't see what I saw."

She shook her head. "You saw what you saw, but it's not murder because you can't kill what's already dead."

Dave's eyes narrowed to confused slits. "Say what now?"

Kelsey nodded. "They're zombies. The living dead."

Dave stared at her for a few moments, dumbfounded by the words she'd uttered, words that made no sense because they were so obviously unconnected to anything in the real world. Any attempt to analyze what she'd said in hopes of ferreting out some hidden layer of truth lurking beneath the absurdity felt like an exercise in futility.

It was almost as if she was speaking some unknown foreign language, one that sounded like an almost recognizable derivation of profoundly bastardized English.

Kelsey must have sensed his skepticism because she went on to say, "Dude, I'm being a hundred percent for fucking real here. This isn't a joke or excuse for what I did. These aren't the first zombies to come through our drive-thru."

The furrow in the middle of Dave's brow deepened to the point it was almost like a flesh canyon glued to his fucking forehead. He chewed on his bottom lip some before managing his first utterance in the wake of Kelsey's bizarre claim.

"Huh. Hmm."

Kelsey sneered, shaking her head. "That's all you've got? I tell you that the zombies are real and making late night burger runs and all you can say is hmm?"

Dave shrugged. "Well, no offense, but it's kind of hard to buy, like stock in K-Mart or Toys R Us."

Kelsey groaned. "Buy it or not, whatever. Doesn't change the fact that we've got two rotting corpses we've gotta get rid of right now."

She turned away from him and stalked over to the Honda in what struck him as a huffy, pissed-off manner, leaning in first to peer into the backseat, presumably to check for anyone else lurking out of sight back there. He'd had a pretty clear view of the vehicle's interior while trying to talk to the groaning driver and knew already it was a pointless endeavor. No one other than the now brain-deprived dead men riding up front had been in the car. He didn't bother telling her because for one thing she'd already seen for herself, and also she didn't seem in a mood to put much stock in anything he said.

Which was kind of wild coming from a shotgun-toting crazy chick who believed zombies were riding around in cars and ordering—or attempting to order—shitty burgers from shitty fast-food joints.

Seeing that the back was empty, she went around to the driver's side, slipping in between the car and the drive-thru window, from which the dead driver's lower half was still hanging. She set the shotgun on the roof of the Honda and grimaced in obvious disgust as she had to wedge herself between the dangling corpse and door to lean in through the window and reach for something below the level of the steering wheel.

A moment later, the trunk popped open.

She backed out of the window and leveled a look at Dave so

lethally furious it felt radioactive. He felt his balls shriveling up and was pretty sure he'd just been rendered permanently infertile. When she spoke next it was in a calm but clear and commanding tone. She needed him to stop gawping and come help her.

Dave wanted no part of any of this, but that shotgun on the roof was still in easy reach for her. Also, at this point he didn't know if this was something he could walk away from with no repercussions. She'd blown away two guys with no indication of pangs of conscience. If she could do that, what was to stop her from coming after him later? Maybe she wouldn't, but he'd be looking over his shoulder for a long, long time. Paranoia would be his constant companion. It'd be so bad he might even have to think about leaving town.

He didn't want to leave town.

Hell, he had barely any experience of the world beyond the borders of this misbegotten blot on the map. Drayton Falls was a dump and kind of a nasty place to live, but it was home.

Sighing, he trudged over to the Honda and begrudgingly helped Kelsey extract the first of the so-called zombies from the drive-thru window. They dragged the corpse around to the back of the vehicle where, working together, they wrestled the two-hundred-pound (or thereabouts) dead man off the pavement and into the open trunk. This task was not accomplished without mishap. Dave had gripped the body under the armpits while Kelsey lifted his lower half. On their first attempt, Dave lost his grip and the corpse's torso thumped back down on the ground. This made Dave the target of some scathing derision from Kelsey, but there was also an extra edge of urgency in her tone, which he understood. Time was passing. Too much of it, maybe. Someone else would come along eventually, regardless of the stultifyingly slow pace of business. The last thing he wanted was to get caught in the act of doing shady shit like this. He'd go to prison for sure, probably even for longer than his piece of shit brother.

Despite his extreme reservations about every aspect of this episode of extreme madness in which he seemed inextricably embroiled, the unpleasant reality was that seeing this nasty business through to the end was his only obvious path back to the land of semi-sanity. Even more important was the even more obvious necessity of getting it done as quickly as possible. Which is to say he was in perhaps too much of an anxious hurry when he knelt to reach for the corpse again and plunged a hand directly into the gaping, squishy crater that was all that remained of the top of the dead man's head.

He recoiled at once, holding up his gore-smeared hand as he cringed in disgust. "Oh, fucking gross. Fuck this fucking bullshit, Kelsey. Fuck it right up the fucking ass."

Kelsey glared at him. "Motherfucker, I'm about to ram my arm down your throat like your throat is a toilet and my arm is the fucking plunger, and then I'm gonna pull out your fucking heart and show that worthless lump of shit to you before I fucking feed it back to you. Do you get the picture or do I have to spell it out for you in even clearer fucking terms?"

Dave was still staring at his dripping hand. "What?"

Kelsey screeched.

Dave flicked his hand without thinking about it, splattering Kelsey's face with blood and gooey bits of brain.

This time Kelsey didn't just screech. She *screamed.*

Then she said, "I swear to god ..."

She trailed off, but, really, nothing more needed to be said. He got the point clearly enough without needing it spelled out. Either he could get his shit together or he could join the "zombies" in the trunk.

He flicked more gore off his hand, this time taking care to direct the shotgun-shredded flesh and brains in a different direction. With that taken care of, he got a surer grip on the corpse and, with a lot perspiration-inducing grunting and straining, they were able to dump the dead man in the trunk. At Kelsey's direction, Dave shoved the body as far toward the back as possible.

In the midst of extracting the second dead man from the Honda, they both went stock-still at the sound of an approaching engine. They stood there at the side of the Honda, frozen like deer in headlights, each gripping a portion of the grotesquely dead second corpse as the sound of the engine grew louder.

The section of street right outside the restaurant was still empty, though.

Dave coughed. "Maybe we should, you know, get on with this."

Kelsey's head swiveled slowly toward him. "Good idea, Einstein."

Working at triple-time speed, they finished hauling the second corpse out of the Honda and dragged it heedlessly around to the trunk, the partially obliterated head scraping against asphalt and leaving a bloody trail the whole way. They were just beginning to lift the annoyingly hefty sack of lifeless garbage off the ground when the car they'd heard went zooming by out on the street without slowing for even a second.

They looked at each other.

Dave shivered. "Close call."

Kelsey grunted. "Yeah."

An awkward pause ensued.

Then Dave said, "You think they saw anything?"

Kelsey shrugged. "Who the fuck knows? Let's finish this."

So they did.

Kelsey slammed the trunk lid shut and retrieved the shotgun from the roof of the Honda. She then approached Dave in an aggressive way that made him cringe away from her, holding up his trembling hands in a weak defensive gesture that would be worth exactly nothing against a shell fired from the weapon. The only reason he didn't piss his pants was that the long barrel was pointed at the ground rather than his face.

Her face registered confusion as she pulled up short, stopping with barely more than a foot of separation between their bodies. "The fuck is wrong with you?"

Dave made a nervous sound that wasn't quite laughter.

Kelsey nodded. "I get it. It's my raw, animal sexuality. You're not used to it. It's intimidating. But you better pull yourself together, cockface, because we're not done yet." She clapped a hand against his shoulder, squeezing it. "We need this car out of sight. Go park it behind the dumpster out back. You hear me? *Behind* it, not in front of it. Got it?"

Dave frowned. "Um ..."

She squeezed his shoulder harder. "Got it?"

He nodded. "Yeah."

She stopped squeezing his shoulder and slapped him on the arm. "Go on, get it done." She started moving away from him, retreating toward the restaurant's side entrance. "I've got a call to make. Get back inside as soon as you're done."

She turned away from him and went on inside.

Once she was gone, he felt a little weird standing outside alone in the empty, quiet parking lot. If not for the trail of blood and brains on the ground, it'd be easy to believe none of what had just transpired had actually happened. He found he could breathe with greater ease again, the tension that had gripped him in the face of Kelsey's state of high agitation slipping away. His hands shook as his mind replayed the gruesome memories of those moments of explosive violence. Before tonight, he'd only ever seen things like that in movies.

Sometimes in zombie movies.

He frowned.

Was it possible Kelsey had told the truth about the dead men currently filling the trunk of the Honda? The idea of shambling, reanimated ghouls existing in real life was something he would dismiss as an absurd impossibility under ordinary circumstances. The rational side of him still wanted to side with this view of things, but in reviewing what he could recall of the groaning man's appearance and behavior in the minutes prior to his brain-splattering demise, he recognized that it was possible to describe it as, well ... zombie-like. The absence of articulate speech, that unnaturally gray skin pallor, the profound confusion regarding the basic mechanics of motor vehicle operation, and so on. And for what reason had he tried crawling in through the drive-thru window?

Robbing the place was one possibility.

A ravenous desire to claw open Dave's stomach and feast on his steaming intestines was maybe another one.

"*Hey!*"

Dave yelped as he again nearly leaped out of his skin.

Kelsey was scowling at him from the drive-thru window, a cordless phone gripped in her right hand. "Why are you just standing there, you fucking dope? Get the car out of sight."

Dave nodded. "Sorry. I'll do it right now."

She watched him as he entered the Honda from the passenger side and clambered over the middle console. In his hurry to slide in behind the wheel, his right foot kicked the shifter, knocking it out of park and into drive. Because the car's engine had been on the entire time, it started rolling forward before Dave could finish situating himself in the seat. He screeched in alarm as he seized hold of the steering wheel, Kelsey's burst of wild laughter from the drive-thru providing a taunting counterpoint.

As he drove around the front of the restaurant and circled toward the back, his nose wrinkled in disgust at the oppressively stale atmosphere inside the car. Beneath the musty odor was a faint sour sweetness. The dumpster out back had just come into view when it hit him that the cloying odor was a death smell. More evidence in support of Kelsey's zombie assertions?

Maybe.

The dumpster was in a corner at the back of the restaurant's rear parking area. Behind it was a stand of trees looming tall and imposing in the darkness. Dave's own car was parked in a space near the dumpster, alongside Kelsey's multi-hued Chevette. The automotive relic's original paint job had faded decades ago, with the current rainbow of colors adorning its exterior these days a result of many inexpertly applied layers of spray paint.

Once again, a fleeting rebellious thought crossed his mind. He didn't have to continue participating in this ongoing conspiracy to cover up a double homicide. His car was right there. His keys were in his pocket. He could hop out right now and go. Instead of doing that, he wedged the Honda in behind the dumpster, cut the engine, got out, and started moving toward the restaurant.

The idea of driving away was a nice fantasy but that was all it was. He rejected it for the same reasons he had the first time it crossed his mind, only now he understood it was even less feasible than it'd been before. Just by driving the car this little bit, he'd left his fingerprints and DNA traces inside it. Maybe that had been Kelsey's subtle way of further ensuring his silent cooperation, though he wasn't sure she was capable of that level of diabolical deviousness. Either way, the result was the same. She could threaten to point the finger at him if he didn't cooperate fully with her every instruction.

All in all, Dave was having a wide range of regrets about having reentered the workforce.

As soon as he was back inside, Kelsey locked up and turned off most of the interior lighting. Only the lights behind the counter and down the short hallway toward the back were still in operation. He saw she'd wheeled out a mop and bucket and parked it in the vicinity of the drive-thru station. She'd also gotten out a pile of rags and several bottles of industrial cleaning fluid.

She smirked when she saw the look on his face. "Did you think we were gonna leave zombie gunk all over the fucking place?"

He shrugged. "I guess not. So are we closed now?"

She nodded. "Yeah, but just for however long it takes to eradicate all traces of zombie carnage, which shouldn't take more than an hour if we work fast. Then we'll open back up."

Dave sighed. "Okay, but, like, you should know I'll be exploring other career options after this."

Kelsey laughed.

Dave frowned. "What's funny about that?"

She was still laughing. "Randall showed me the application you filled out. Your resume was, shall we say, not that fucking impressive."

Dave wanted to argue with her but found he could not.

After all, she wasn't wrong.

They set about the nasty work of cleaning up all the blood and gruel and had been at it for around half an hour by the time Randall Farnsworth pulled up in his GTO and banged on the side door. Kelsey dropped the bloody rags in her yellow-gloved hands and ran to the door, yanking on the zip cord at her waist to slide the key in the lock and let their boss in.

He questioned Kelsey about the incident, his demeanor far calmer than Dave had anticipated. Nothing she said appeared to surprise or alarm him. He made subdued noises of acknowledgement and occasionally nodded as she told him all about it. Throughout it all, Dave's sense of astonished confusion continued to grow. Farnsworth gave not the slightest indication of finding anything unusual about the incident.

Randall praised Kelsey for her decisive action, telling her she'd get the usual bonus in her next paycheck.

Then he turned his attention to Dave, an inquisitive eyebrow going up as he gave his new employee's face a discomfiting level of attention. "You okay, kid? Not too shook up?"

Dave shrugged. "I guess."

He didn't know what else to say to a question as crazy as that.

Of course he wasn't "okay".

But he had an idea it might not be smart to admit it.

Randall studied his face for another tensely silent moment. Then he broke out in a big, jovial smile and clapped Dave on the shoulder. "Yeah, you'll be fine. If it makes you feel any better, you'll get a bonus, too, but trust me, kid, it's totally not a big deal. There was a chemical spill out this way years and years ago. It got hushed up, never made the news. We'll go weeks or sometimes even months without an incident, but every now and then you get one of these situations where somebody dies and comes back with a newly acquired taste for human flesh. It was just your bad luck it happened your first night."

Dave nodded. "I see."

He didn't see. Not at fucking all.

But by then the manager's attention had shifted back to Kelsey. "I'll have a crew out here before sunrise to take the car away. You need anything else from me or are we good to go?"

Kelsey smiled. "All good, sir. We've got it handled."

"Good to hear it." The manager started backing up toward the side entrance, pointing a finger Dave's way as he pushed the door open. "Hang in there, kid. You survived your first-day trial by fire. It's all downhill from here."

And with that, he went out the door, hopped back in his GTO, and sped away.

As soon as he was gone, Kelsey took Dave by the hand and led him to the storeroom in back, closing the door as soon as they were inside. He was already a bit flustered by the semi-intimate physical contact, but his jaw almost hit the floor when she pulled off her uniform smock and the shirt beneath it and cast them aside. Next she unsnapped her black bra, teasingly holding the cups against her breasts for a moment before allowing the lacy fabric to slip from her fingers.

She smirked at his flabbergasted expression. "Stop gawking and get undressed. I've gotta get this out of my system before we get back to cleaning."

Despite the admonition, Dave gawked a little longer, but he did finally manage to shed his grungy clothes. He was nervous and intensely self-conscious, but he correctly surmised he wasn't being given a choice here. Once he was nude, Kelsey mounted up, riding him hard atop a large box of kitchen supplies. After a frenzied few minutes, she left Dave gasping for breath and stunned by the sudden and unexpected utter obliteration of his virginity.

A short while later, they collected themselves, got dressed, and returned to the messy job of cleaning up zombie brains. They worked in silence for the most part, the only sounds those produced by the squirting of cleaner bottles and the wet slap of the mop. By the time they were nearly done, Dave's every thought was still centered around the frenzied coupling in the storeroom. He could still hardly believe it had happened and more than once had to mentally pause and assure himself it was a real thing he'd experienced and not simply some extra-vivid fantasy of the sort he used to torture himself with during long days in school.

Unlike the sexy cheerleaders he'd dreamed about while sitting at the back of so many classrooms and ignoring the relentless droning of teachers, this girl was not only attainable, he'd *attained* her. Except saying it that way wasn't exactly right, because it made it sound like he'd played an active role in the seduction, when all he'd really done was to lie back and let it happen. Everything felt different now, the world brighter, more vibrant and vital, the air itself thrumming with an ever-present electrical current he'd somehow been oblivious to his entire life. He was astounded by how thoroughly the mere act of being inside a woman for the first time could change his perspective on seemingly *everything*.

Kelsey slapped a wet, bloodstained cloth against the counter. "Stop it."

From his squatting position on the floor, Dave glanced up at her, confusion etched in his features. "Huh? Stop what?"

She rolled her eyes. "That moony look. Like you're already in love with me after one fuck."

A hot flush reddened Dave's cheeks. "Um, I, uh …um …"

All he could do was stammer as the flush intensified, sweat forming in his armpits as he was overcome with a case of embarrassment so extreme it scared him. Was it possible to die from embarrassment? He wasn't sure, but his heart was beating so hard simply keeling over didn't feel like the remote possibility it should be at his young age.

Kelsey sighed. "I'm going to regret this, I see. Fuck me." She scowled, shaking her head at Dave's sudden sharp intake of breath. "Jesus. Not literally. Not right now, anyway. Look, I was just all riled up from what happened. Shooting those dead fucks. The violence. The blood. The fucking adrenaline." She shrugged. "I just needed to blow off some steam. You know?"

Dave picked a small skull fragment off the floor, frowned as he studied its smooth and sharp-edged contours a moment, then dumped it in the bucket at his feet. "Yeah," he said, nodding as he looked at her again. "I get it. I just … it was so great."

This time, for once, Kelsey didn't snap back with a snide remark. She held his gaze in a frank way that set his heart to racing again. Then, for a fraction of a second so brief it might only have been an illusion, the tiniest hint of a smile shaded the edges of her mouth.

She shrugged. "I guess I've had worse."

And that was all they said about it until much later.

They lapsed back into silence as they finished cleaning up.

Kelsey tied a knot in the big black garbage back into which they'd deposited all the physical remnants of the dead man's head along with all the bloody rags. She unlocked the side door and together they walked out to the dumpster in back, where Kelsey shoved the bag through one of the Honda's open windows.

On the way back into the restaurant, Dave cleared his throat and said, "So this happens often enough that Randall has a regular crew he sends out here to get rid of the evidence?"

Kelsey nodded. "Yeah, sort of. It's actually Mr. Conroy's people."

Dave frowned. "Who the fuck is Mr. Conroy?"

"The guy who owns Big Fiesta Burgers." She grunted, then smiled. "Owns anything of any real value out this way. Not that anything out here is worth that much. There's a chop shop for the cars. They all get disassembled, the parts sold."

"What happens to the bodies?"

She laughed. "Randall handles that personally. Let's just say there's a reason people call him 'Hacksaw'."

Dave made a thoughtful noise. "Hmm. For cutting up bodies."

Kelsey cackled. "Nothing gets past you."

Once they were back inside, they washed up a final time and Kelsey reopened the restaurant, flipping on the interior and exterior lights. Two more cars came through the drive-thru during the final two hours of Dave's first shift, both loaded with late night drunks who were obnoxious but not zombies.

At the end of their shift, they walked out back together.

Dave muttered an awkward good night and started moving toward his car.

"Wait."

He glanced back at Kelsey, an eyebrow arched. "Yeah?"

She nodded at his trashy Pinto. "Do you really sleep in that thing? Randall says you do."

Dave grimaced, a tinge of embarrassment creeping into his cheeks again. "For now. Until I can save up some money and get a place."

"That's pathetic."

Dave didn't know what to say to that. Being called pathetic wasn't a new experience. It'd happened countless thousands of times over the years, so often it shouldn't sting quite so much as it did now.

He shoved his hands in his pockets and looked at the ground. "Yeah."

Kelsey groaned. "Fuck it. You can stay with me a while."

His eyes lit up with a pitiful flicker of hopefulness. "Really?"

She nodded. "I'm impulsive sometimes. I don't know if you've noticed." She opened the door of her own car and looked at him over the roof. "Follow my shit-heap in your shit-heap. Get moving before I change my mind."

She dropped into her car and shut the door before he could say anything else, firing the rattling engine up and beginning the process of backing out of her space. Dave, still standing outside his own car at that point, scrambled to get his door open and hurry after her. After a harrowing first few moments of zipping around the bends of the curvy back road, he caught up to Kelsey and a short while later they arrived at her single-wide trailer in the Starry Skies trailer park. Dave stayed with her that night and the next night as well. And then the one after that and then the night after that and so on. What began as a casual arrangement neither party viewed as all that serious kept going on and on, slowly solidifying into something more substantial. Whenever anyone asks regarding their official status, these days Kelsey shrugs and admits that they are "sort of" living together.

One night several months into Dave's employment with Big Fiesta Burgers, the evening's first customer didn't show up until more than three hours into his shift. When the alert tone sounded in his headset, he glanced at the fuzzy black-and-white image on the monitor. As always, the shitty quality of the monitoring equipment made it difficult to know exactly what the driver looked like. If they were moving around at all, the camera transformed their heads into amorphous, blurry blobs, whereas if they remained relatively still, you could get some sense of the general shape of their faces.

In this case, the guy behind the steering wheel was kind of bouncing around in a weird state of agitation, making goofy faces and noises, his features coming into semi-focus for only fleeting instants here and there. Those flashing fractional seconds of relative faint clarity wouldn't have meant anything had the driver been virtually anyone else, but this time they were all Dave needed to recognize the person sitting at the speaker pole out back.

Sensing the shift in his demeanor, Kelsey looked up at him from her kneeling position in front of him and wiped her mouth with the back of a hand. "Somebody here?"

Dave felt like he had a golf ball lined with razor blades lodged in his throat.

All he could do was nod.

The guy behind the wheel of the car leaned out the window and banged on the speaker pole.

Kelsey frowned. "Who is it?"

Dave grimaced. "My fucking brother."

After tucking his junk away and zipping up his pants, Kelsey got to her feet without a word and walked away, presumably in

23

anticipation of preparing some fast fucking food for the first time all night.

Dave raised a hand to his headset to press the talk button, but before he could do that, Gary Shepherd gave up trying to talk to him through the speaker, hit the gas, and came to a screeching halt outside the drive-thru window approximately one second later.

He leered at Dave, leaning out the window of his car as he continued making bizarre faces, crossing his eyes and twisting his features to convey an impression of imbecilic derangement. Whether this was just goofing around on his part or a true reflection of his mental state was hard to say. Whatever the case, it was clearly tinged with a generous helping of drug-fueled mania. Dave couldn't help noting the presence of what looked suspiciously like pieces of a mutilated cow in the back of his brother's car.

"What are you doing here, Gary? You're kind of out of your way, aren't you?"

Gary cackled. "Shit, man, I heard this wild fuckin' rumor my dumbass little bro was working at a crappy Mexican place out in the boonies. I had to come check that shit out for myself because I couldn't believe it, yo. Like, me and the folks thought you were dead or some shit, it'd been so long since you showed your ugly fuckin' mug around our side of town. So the other day I went down to the car wash and talked to your old butt buddy Fat Bob, who told me about your new gig. Like I said, I couldn't fuckin' believe it but turns out it was the real straight dope because here you are, big as life and uglier than ever. Ain't that some shit."

Dave nodded.

That was some shit, all right. Straight up.

Gary's entire greeting speech was delivered without a single pause, in one breathless outburst. It was like listening to a sped-up recording of his normal speaking voice. Dave was now positive beyond any doubt drugs were a major motivating factor here, perhaps a variety of them. From the way the jackass was acting, he might even be back on the Belgian toad venom, a hunch strongly supported by the apparent evidence of a new case of cattle mutilation.

Dave sighed. "Well, now you've seen it for yourself, so maybe go ahead and move along, eh?"

Gary stopped making the goofy faces, his expression turning hard. It was the look of a recidivist felon who'd fully reembraced all his old bad habits. "I ain't goin' anywhere until you give me some food, boy.

Gots me a case of the mad munchies, bro. I feel like if I don't get somethin' in my belly real fuckin' soon, I might just go crazy, you dig?" At that point, he tilted his head sideways, crossed his eyes again, and made another of his lunatic faces. Then he howled laughter, repeatedly slapping the steering wheel hard enough to make it vibrate. Another abrupt hardening of his expression came next. "You bein' my bro and all, I figure I should get the family discount." He laughed again. "Give me some free grub, bitch!"

More hard slapping of the steering wheel ensued.

Dave felt a presence behind him.

Gary abruptly sobered, tilting his head again as his brow furrowed. "Yo, bro, who's the skank? That your girlfriend?" He leaned back in his seat and grabbed his crotch, leering at them. "She ain't much to look at, but I've seen worse. You gotta share with your big brother, bro. Tell that skinny bitch to get out here and ride my dong!"

Keeping her hands below Gary's line of sight, Kelsey pressed something into Dave's hands, leaning close to whisper in his ear. "I see a zombie, don't you?"

For the briefest of moments, Dave was horrified.

Then he began to smile. "Yes, I think I do."

He lifted the shotgun and aimed it at his deranged brother through the open drive-thru window.

Gary howled more laughter when he saw the muzzle of the shotgun pointed at his face. "Aw, shit! Little Davey's got hisself a pew-pew toy. Put that thing down, son. You ain't got the—"

Dave squeezed the trigger.

One of his life's greatest annoyances disappeared in a hazy red mist of gore.

As Dave set the shotgun on the counter and rushed outside to seize control of the car—which had started slowly rolling away from the drive-thru—Kelsey made a phone call.

The call connected.

She had a brief conversation, hanging up less than a minute later.

A crew from the chop shop was on the way.

CLASS
REUNION
SLAUGHTER

PREAMBLE

YOU KNOW THAT OLD CLICHÉ about high school being the best years of your life, right? It's mostly a lie, of course, a big old sack of bullshit myth propagated by movies and fuzzy nostalgia. For a select few among us, it might actually be true, and I bet most of you could hazard a guess who I mean. The good-looking popular kids. Football players and cheerleaders. The Homecoming Queen and King. Maybe a class clown or two who had ordinary looks but made everybody laugh and ingratiated himself—or herself—with the star quarterback or head cheerleader.

Yeah, you know, because every American high school going back at least a hundred years has had its "in" crowd, and in almost every case the makeup of that group is largely the same. Maybe it's different in strict religious or military prep schools, but I wouldn't know about that because, like most of you, I went to regular old public high school, where the social hierarchy and the specific type of cruelty it can foster never changes.

I'm referring here, of course, to the standard bullying and

ostracization of awkward or "different" kids that occurs in such environments, but would you believe me if I told you that sometimes even the most exalted members of the in crowd can be haunted by their high school experience? Because sometimes bad things can happen to *anyone* who's young and not yet in possession of a fully formed sense of right and wrong.

Sometimes those things are *very* bad.

Tragic, even.

The tale I'm about to tell you involves one of those situations, and it happened right here in Drayton Falls. And because Drayton Falls is the kind of town it is, a place that actively fuels and nurtures the evil and the macabre, it was so much more horrific than most similar stories from other places you've heard.

So, sit down by the fire here with me and crack a cold one or two, because this one's gonna get bloody.

ONE

AFTER TWENTY-FIVE YEARS OF anonymous exile in a large city hundreds of miles away, Christopher Schaefer had come home to Drayton Falls. Sitting behind the wheel of his eleven-year-old Chevy Cruz, he was assailed by a mix of strong emotions as he stared at the entrance to the drab-looking building once housing Drayton High. There was a newer, far more modern high school serving the community now. That much nicer building was barely more than a mile down the road.

These changes were new knowledge for Christopher, who'd remained almost entirely unaware of changes and developments in the town of his birth for the past quarter century. He was that rare animal, a Drayton Falls native who fled the dead-end town after graduation and never came back.

Until now, that is.

A whole new generation of Folly kids had come of age and entered adulthood in the time he'd been away. And now some of that generation's own kids were entering school. It was crazy to think about. All that time gone in what seemed like a flash. It seemed like yesterday he'd been roaming those halls, strutting around like the cock of the walk, a big and muscular handsome football star who scored with all the hottest chicks. He was treated like a king because he was one. Because his dad was rich by local standards, he had the nicest, flashiest car of anyone in school, a cherry red Corvette. Except for some of the loser nerds he'd bullied, as decreed by unofficial tradition, he was beloved by everyone.

Well … maybe not quite everyone.

Christopher screwed the cap off the pint bottle of Jack Daniel's he'd purchased at Conroy Liquors and Wine not even twenty minutes earlier and took a deep slug of whiskey. Then he stared at the bottle and frowned because here was another weird-to-think-about thing. He hadn't legally been able to buy alcohol the last time he'd been in this dump of a town and now here he was, middle-aged, able to buy booze without fuss any time he damn well pleased.

They'd had some high old times back then, he and his football buddies and all the other members of the in-crowd. All those weekend keg parties were as legendary as their gridiron heroics. It was a glorious time for many who ran in their circles.

What most people hadn't known back then, even his closest friends, was that he'd existed in a state of secret dread throughout senior year, knowing that graduation would bring a permanent end to his reign as the unofficial king of the Drayton Falls youth community. His plan to leave town and never look back was formulated over Christmas break that year, during which he stewed over some things that had happened that fall. Things that came closer than he liked to admit to ruining his life forever. They'd been dealt with, seemingly, but he couldn't stop obsessing over the idea they'd come back to bite him eventually if he stayed.

So Christopher stuck to his secret plan and drove off into the sunset after graduation.

For the longest time, he'd believed he would never return. Thoughts of seeing his old stomping grounds were the furthest thing from his mind for years and years. His life in the big city wasn't glamorous or exciting, but at least he'd never felt burdened by the weight of his past there. There was no one or anything around to remind him of high school. He was no longer covered in glory, but he was content.

Or so he told himself for a long time. There was no inkling of this ever changing until some of his old buddies got together and hired a private detective to track him down. Once they'd located him, they got in touch and started begging him to come to their twenty-fifth reunion. All the guys told him it just wouldn't be the same without him there. He *had* to come. Initially he resisted, but they didn't give up and eventually wore him down.

And now here he was, minutes away from seeing faces he'd last seen a lifetime ago. The prospect was intimidating, largely because he didn't feel like he was simply an older version of the person he'd been in those old days. He felt barely *any* connection to his younger self, like he'd become a different person entirely, which had kind of been the goal.

When he tried to imagine swilling beers with the old gang, he simply couldn't picture it. He had a sense of how the rest of them would be. Laughing and cutting up, telling the same old jokes and stories. None of them had ever left Drayton Falls and still saw each other all the time. They had decades of shared experiences. Backyard barbecues. Family get-togethers. Baby showers and weddings. Hanging out at the local bars and watching football games. Super Bowl parties and holidays.

All that shit.

Christopher, the person he'd become in the long interim, would be a stranger in their midst.

He took another big gulp of whiskey and put the cap back on the bottle, tucking it away inside his jacket as he continued eyeing the school with trepidation.

He reached for the door handle and hesitated.

This is a big fucking mistake, an inner voice piped up. *There's still time to turn around and leave.*

He lingered a few extra minutes in the car. Up to this point, he'd felt entirely committed to being here. It'd be ridiculous to come all this way and just leave without ever going inside or seeing anyone.

Except … was it?

There'd be a strange kind of symmetry to doing a thing like that, an echo of his vanishment into self-exile all those years ago. It'd almost be kind of funny, although he suspected his old friends might disagree.

In fact, they'd probably be pretty fucking angry.

Christopher sighed and let his head fall back against the headrest. Despite this moment of temptation, he knew he would not surrender to the impulse. As he'd told his wife before heading out on his trip, he was committed to this being the one and only time he'd ever return to Drayton Falls. When he left here again tomorrow, it would be forever. He needed to set aside his worries and go inside and make peace with his past.

He figured he'd have a good time once he got inside and was able to relax after a few minutes and a few more drinks.

Later on, he'd be glad he'd done it.

Probably.

The thing still giving him pause was the possible presence of one person in particular. A person he'd done wrong in an especially egregious way early on in that fraught senior year. Wrong in a way that set all the rest of the ensuing nastiness in motion. That person being here tonight didn't seem likely for multiple reasons, but it wasn't out of the realm of possibility.

Still … twenty-five fucking years.

It was a long goddamn time and who in their right mind would hold onto a grudge for that long?

Christopher smirked and shook his head.

Go on inside, you old chickenshit.

He reached for the door handle again.

And that was when the person who'd been hiding in his backseat since his stop at Conroy Liquors and Wine sat up and looped the length of razor wire around his throat. The assailant's thick leather gloves provided protection from personal injury as the wire was drawn tight against Christopher's neck, cutting into his skin and drawing out a line of bright red blood almost instantly.

Christopher realized how much trouble he was in within about one second. His eyes popped open wide and his heart felt like it was the size of a bowling ball as it pounded heavily in his chest. He felt the warm blood pool in the hollow of his throat and then go sliding downward, staining the nice new shirt he'd bought for the occasion. His thoughts were a mad, confused scramble, but at the center of it all was a clear awareness he was about to die if he didn't do something. He tried pushing his fingers up under the length of wire to pry it away from his neck before it could open one of the big veins and finish him, but this proved an impossible task. The wire was too tight and drawing tighter by the moment. His fingers were getting sliced up and the blood was making the wire too slippery to grasp anyway.

His bulging eyes flicked to the rearview in hopes of catching a glimpse of his killer. Because that was how he was already thinking of the unknown person in the back of his car. His killer. This was a battle he was already destined to lose because he was at a disadvantage so profound it made fighting back an impossibility. The assailant was not in full view from this angle, but a portion of the person's head was visible above the headrest. His killer was wearing a black ski mask, but something about those eyes was familiar. The long hair protruding from the bottom of the mask provided an additional clue.

A spark of recognition flared inside Christopher. He didn't need to see this person's face to know who was killing him. Along with this insight came the bitter knowledge that he'd been tragically wrong about one thing above all others.

Not all grudges fade away with time.

Some last forever.

The wire kept pulling tighter against his neck, the blood flowing faster and faster. Despite recognizing the seeming hopelessness of his situation, the primal instinct to survive wasn't yet dead inside him. Only death itself could extinguish it, and as long as his heart was still beating, he had at least a chance. An infinitesimal one, yes, but he was determined to go down fighting.

Abandoning his useless attempts to pull the wire away from his neck, he reached into his jacket pocket with shaking fingers coated in blood and pulled out the mostly full pint bottle of Jack Daniels. He'd only taken a couple of slugs from it, meaning it possibly still had enough heft to it to wield as an effective weapon. The bottle came out of his pocket and he held it gripped in his bloody hand as tightly as he could manage. There was a better than even chance it would go sliding out of his fingers the instant he tried to swing it at his attacker, but he had to try.

Logic told him his only hope was to play possum and convince the attacker the job was already done. He needed to relax his body and go as still as possible. The idea was terrifying because his instincts were telling him to keep fighting, to not quit for even a second as long as he still had breath in his body. Resisting this impulse was like fighting against a force of nature, like walking head-on into hurricane-force winds, but he did it anyway, convinced now it was his only hope. He needed the killer to relax and loosen that wire, allow him the range of motion he needed to twist around and attack.

He went as still as a statue.

The assailant held the wire tight a few seconds longer, drew it even tighter for a moment or two as a froth of bloody spittle dribbled from the corners of Christopher's mouth. His head was swimming as his vision went in and out of focus. For a few fuzzy moments there, he was certain his desperate gambit had failed, that he wouldn't even get a chance to fight back.

Then he heard the attacker let out a breath.

An instant later, the wire went slack against his neck, though it still remained embedded in his skin. As soon he felt this happen, Christopher gathered every remaining ounce of his strength still at his disposal and twisted around in his seat, ignoring the way the wire cut into his skin again, drawing out another thin sheet of blood. One of his feet slid backward into the footwell beneath the steering wheel, but he was able to balance a knee on the edge of the seat and swing the bottle around.

The attacker glimpsed the oncoming bottle a second too late, making an unsuccessful attempt to dodge out of the way. Never in his life had Christopher heard a sound as satisfying as the loud crack of the glass shattering against the side of the assailant's head. The attacker relinquished their grip on the ends of the razor wire and pitched backward, moaning in pain.

An electric thrill of triumph sizzled through every nerve ending in Christopher's body. He ripped the wire away from his neck and cast it aside. His heart was still slamming from the waves of adrenaline-fueled terror continuing to crash over him like tsunami surges, but soon the feeling was joined by an almost equally powerful sense of rage. He didn't deserve to die for stupid bullshit he'd done as a kid. A thing he'd always regretted and tried to use as motivation to become a better person. Not that any of that mattered now. Not after this. Not after coming so close to checking out forever and never getting back home again, never seeing his beautiful wife and kid again.

That rage-fueled part of him wanted to climb into the backseat and finish the job on his assailant. To end the threat forever. What swayed him against it, in the end, was the knowledge that he was still in a deeply vulnerable position. The assailant was stunned, but how long would that last?

More importantly, he was badly wounded. Blood was still flowing from the deep slice in his neck.

He needed help. Emergency medical treatment.

What he needed to do was get out of this fucking blood-splattered car and run into the building. He'd alert his old classmates to the danger and let them take over. They'd call the cops, summon an ambulance, provide first aid to make sure he didn't bleed out.

Shoving the rage down, he turned around in the seat again and reached for the door handle. His slippery fingers were just beginning to curl around it when the attacker abruptly snapped out of their stupor and lunged forward, this time to drive the point of a large hunting knife deep into the side of his neck.

Christopher experienced a moment of the most intense anguish he'd ever known because in that instant he knew the fight truly was over. He'd had his chance to prevail and had blown it. The length of steel was lodged too far inside his flesh. The killer held it there a moment longer, allowing him more time to fully appreciate the bleak finality and terrifying hopelessness of what he was facing.

Then the killer laughed softly and whispered his name, reminding him of a long ago promise to exact revenge one day.

A promise that had now been fulfilled.

The killer ripped the blade out of Christopher's neck, opening his carotid and sending a bright splash of blood arcing across the windshield. After Christopher had slumped in his seat and breathed his last, the killer grabbed hold of him and wrestled him into the backseat.

There was still work to be done.

More measures of long-delayed revenge to exact, but the part of it involving Christopher was still not quite finished.

Out of the killer's bag of shiny new murder toys came a heavy meat cleaver, purchased only the day before at a cutlery store.

Up went the cleaver and down it came.

Up and down. Up and down.

Again and again.

Chop, chop, chop.

Blood spraying everywhere.

Until the job, at last, was done.

This one, anyway.

TWO

A BAND ON A CHINTZY little stage was playing something Duncan Miller needed several moments to recognize as a cover of a song by Blink-182. The song had been popular the year before graduation. A handful of people were dancing to it in front of the stage, though mostly not with a lot of discernible enthusiasm. The sole exception to that was one couple who were throwing their bodies around like they were still eighteen years old. The woman-half of the couple had a lithe, athletic figure and looked smashing in her low-cut yellow dress, with her long blonde hair flying wildly all about. Her moves were so good she looked like a pro dancer in a music video. The guy matched her enthusiasm if not quite her grace.

They were Stacy Nelson and Warn Griggs.

Back in the day, they'd been Drayton High's most hot and heavy couple, just constantly all over each other to an obnoxious degree. After a while, when they had classes together, teachers began making them sit on opposite sides of the room in order to maintain some semblance of decorum while class was in session. Before that, there'd been times when it seemed they were on the verge of engaging in actual sex while a teacher was in the middle of giving a lecture. No amount of stern scolding ever made a difference, so separation became the only option.

After graduation, they broke up and eventually married other people, separately raising families in apparent contentment, their adolescent love affair consigned to the past without regret. Or so it'd always seemed until tonight. Duncan couldn't recall seeing them dance together like this at previous reunions, although to be fair he'd skipped the twenty-year bash. Maybe they'd gotten up to similar shenanigans that time. Who knew?

The Blink-182 song came to a discordant end and the band immediately launched into another old pop-punk anthem. Drayton High's one-time most notorious couple never missed a beat, just kept dancing together in that same high-energy way, seizing occasional opportunities to grind against each other in a way that decidedly did not match the rhythm of the song.

One of Duncan's closest friends from high school, a guy he still hung out with on a semi-regular basis, was Phil Nunnally. Detaching himself from a conversation with a group of former jocks, Phil made his way over to the open bar, where Duncan had stationed himself since his arrival, departing the vicinity only occasionally for trips to the bathroom.

Phil frowned as he eyed the way Duncan was holding up his phone.

"Shit, man, are you recording them?"

Duncan chuckled, nodding. "Yep."

Phil glanced out toward the sparsely populated area in front of the little stage where people were dancing. "You're not gonna do anything crazy, are you? Because posting a video like that on Facebook or the Gram would be like dropping a nuclear bomb on both their marriages."

Duncan laughed. "Probably not. I'm not a total bastard. Doesn't mean I might not torture them with it some before the night's over."

He hit the button to end the recording and dropped the phone in his hip pocket.

"Any sign of Chris yet?" Phil asked him.

Duncan shook his head. "Not yet."

His position near the bar was also adjacent to the gymnasium's entrance, which meant he was among the first to see anyone entering or leaving. Aside from the gals dispensing ID badges at the table in the hallway, that is.

Phil groaned and rolled his eyes. "You watch. Dude's gonna flake. I bet we don't see him at all tonight."

Duncan wanted to believe Phil was wrong on that count. They'd all been looking forward to seeing the long-absent unofficial former leader of their old gang for the first time in forever. After disappearing without explanation the day after graduation, he'd gone off-radar, effectively sealing himself off from all his old high school pals and acquaintances, leaving even his family in the dark.

Tonight was meant to be the night when that was finally supposed to change, the night when everyone would come together again, but the longer Chris remained a no-show, the more likely Phil's gloomy prediction seemed. They'd all talked about it in the weeks and final days leading up to the event, debating the relative likelihood of another unexplained disappearing act.

Duncan nodded to the group of old football players Phil had been jawing with before swinging over to talk to him. "What's Jason saying about it?"

He was referring to Jason Farnsworth, a one-time offensive lineman who was now a city councilman. It was Jason who'd taken the lead in the renewed search for Christopher several months ago, hiring the detective who'd finally tracked the man down.

Phil frowned. "Says the last he heard Chris was in town and on his way here, but that was already an hour ago. He's tried calling and texting the guy a few times since then, but he's not answering."

Duncan took a big gulp from the beer he'd only been nursing while recording the amorous couple. "Huh. That doesn't sound good. Maybe he got cold feet all of a sudden."

Phil nodded. "That's sort of what we're all thinking." His appeared to think about something. "Do you know that for a long time I figured the guy was dead? It was the only thing I could think of that made sense. Like maybe he drove off on some adventure after graduation, just some wild impulse, never meaning to be gone forever, but then he got himself in trouble and wound up killed, body buried out in the wilderness or wherever. Hell, even his folks didn't know where he was or what happened. Or so they always told everybody, though I guess maybe they knew and were keeping the truth to themselves."

Duncan's own thoughts on the subject had often followed a

similar course over the years. That total silence and absolute dearth of information stretching out over such a long period made a grim fate seem very possible. It'd felt like a miracle when he heard the news about him being found. He hadn't been quite as close with Christopher as some of the other guys in their friend circle, but he'd liked him a lot, just like everyone else.

Almost everyone else, anyway.

Phil glanced around in a furtive way that was so specific and familiar it almost made Duncan burst out laughing. He had a hunch he knew what his old friend would say even before the words passed his lips.

"Hey, man, you wanna slip out back and toke up?"

Duncan drained off the last dregs of his beer and gave the empty bottle a shake. "Sure, why not? Just let me grab another beer first."

Phil grunted. "Get one for me too, will ya?"

"Sure thing."

A couple minutes later, after threading their way through the modest crowd at an accelerated and purposeful pace that discouraged attempts at interaction from former classmates, they exited the gym through the rear doors. They were then in the short hallway that separated the boys' and girls' locker rooms and showers. It was a space Duncan had last glimpsed twenty-five years ago, all previous reunions having been held at various off-site venues.

Passing through the hallway unlocked a new batch of forgotten memories, sights and sounds that felt so distant yet so near. Echoes in his mind of guys talking shit in the locker room. The ear-splitting sound of the PE coach's whistle. That annoying squeaking noise sneakers made on the hardwoods. All at once he had an intense sense of how quickly all that time had passed, as if it'd only been a moment or two ago, and it was kind of a drag to contemplate. He could too easily imagine the next twenty-five years passing even faster, the rest of his life—or nearly so—gone in a flash.

Not the most fun thing to think about.

Up to this point, he'd felt only a mild enthusiasm for toking up with Phil, almost as if he were doing it as a courtesy, a grudging way of indulging his friend's nostalgia for a former favorite activity. Now, though, getting high felt like the best possible idea. Beer helped, at least in certain quantities, but there was nothing like weed to chase gloom away. It'd been many years since he'd last smoked, but he remembered the sensations well, how much lighter it'd always made him feel.

They were outside seconds later, standing in the cool evening air after propping the door open with a trashcan as Phil fished a joint of significant girth from an inner pocket of his blazer. Duncan was under the impression that most modern weed aficionados preferred other delivery methods—pipes, edibles, blunts, and so forth—but Phil was nothing if not steadfastly old school.

He dragged a plastic lighter out of a hip pocket, flared up, and took an initial deep drag on the joint, holding the smoke in his lungs with his lips pressed firmly shut before passing it to Duncan.

Duncan accepted the joint and inserted it between his lips, drawing smoke deep into his lungs, filling them up. When he exhaled, the smoke came out in a harsh rush, making his throat feel raw on the way out, a feeling exacerbated by the force of the coughing attack that ensued.

He held the joint outward, pinched between thumb and forefinger, even as he stood bent over and coughing for another few moments.

Phil laughed as he plucked it from his fingers and took another drag, not as deep as his first. "You sound out of practice."

Duncan nodded as he stood up straight again, the coughing fit mostly having subsided. "You could say that, yeah."

The comment elicited louder laughter from Phil, who said, "In that case, prepare to be way higher than you've ever been. This shit is no joke. It's way stronger than the stuff we smoked as kids."

Duncan frowned, eyeing the joint with even greater wariness as Phil again passed it back his way. "Huh. You think maybe you should have warned me about that first?"

Phil grinned and opened his mouth to offer some form of reply—undoubtedly of the sarcastic variety—but before he could get the words out, they were both distracted by a sound of approaching footsteps coming from an unexpected direction, around a corner of the building instead of the open door to the hallway.

Each of their faces bore nearly identical expressions of confusion as a svelte blonde woman with a pleasing figure appeared from around the corner and came striding toward them at a rapid clip. The confusion stemmed in part from the way she was dressed, which was in a vintage Drayton High cheerleading outfit. Her bare legs were smooth and toned like those of an actual cheerleader of high school or college age, but there were a few blemishes here and there one wouldn't expect of a young girl.

The attire was unusual if not entirely out of place. Most of the cheerleaders from their day would probably struggle to squeeze into their old uniforms, but the main thing that confused them was the ski mask. Also unsettling was what looked like splashes of blood on the woman's arms and across the front of her uniform top. Even the long blonde hair protruding from the bottom of the ski mask was spattered with crimson.

Duncan and Phil shared a puzzled glance.

Duncan could already feel the marijuana starting to take hold. His old buddy clearly hadn't lied about the strength of the strain. The encroaching weed buzz made him want to laugh at the incongruous parts of the woman's retro outfit, but he wasn't yet so stoned he didn't feel a stirring of alarm. Was that real blood all over her?

And if so, shouldn't they be running back into the building?

As their gazes returned to the still oncoming faux cheerleader, Phil chortled loud laughter. "Hey, doll, I think you got your dates mixed up. It ain't Halloween yet."

The masked woman stopped in her tracks less than ten feet from where they stood. A black burlap bag was gripped in her right hand. The way the bottom of it sagged suggested the presence of something heavy inside. They saw her red-painted lips stretch wide in a big smile through the mouth hole of the mask.

"I have a surprise for you boys. Do you want to see?"

Phil and Duncan exchanged another frowning glance.

Then Phil looked at her and said, "Sure, babe, show us what you got."

He laughed again.

But Duncan was still frowning.

Had he detected a note of vague familiarity in the timbre of that sweetly musical voice? He wasn't sure, but hearing it triggered a faint sense of unease, as if it had rattled the rusty lock on some long-buried bad memory, an actively suppressed one hidden way back in the remotest recesses of his mind. Though he was unable to immediately link the voice to anyone he knew, it was of a type he'd once associated with certain girls in his senior class who'd been in the Drayton Falls cheer squad. Bubbly and perky, with a tendency to add dramatic emphasis to seemingly random words. In this case, he'd heard that emphasis on three words—*I*, *surprise*, and *see*.

A sense of frustration intruded as he realized the buzz from the turbo-charged strain of THC circulating in his system was growing stronger by the moment, hampering his ability to think clearly and unlock the pleasant thing his brain was hiding from him. One thing the weed did not impede was his rapidly growing feeling of alarm.

The woman opened the black bag, squatted on her haunches, and started rooting around inside it, an action that produced a clanking sound of metallic objects bumping against one another. During these moments, her attention was focused only on the contents of her bag.

Duncan leaned close to Phil and nudged him with an elbow, addressing him in an urgent whisper. "Something feels fucked here. We should go inside. Like, right now."

Phil was still staring at the masked woman as he took another deep drag on the joint. He held the smoke in his lungs another few moments as Duncan pulled on his arm in an attempt to steer him back toward the open door behind them. Phil shrugged him off as he exhaled another big cloud of smoke.

"Relax, dude, this chick is hot. I mean, yeah, who knows what the face looks like, but check out the bitchin' bod."

The woman in the cheerleader outfit chuckled.

Duncan realized she'd clearly heard Phil's every word because he was using his normal speaking voice. In addition to lowering his inhibitions, the weed was causing an apparent mental regression on his friend's part. Phil was a smart guy who owned a moderately successful business. When conversing with him in virtually any other setting under normal circumstances, he sounded like the intelligent middle-aged adult he actually was, whereas right now he sounded like he was a teenager again.

The woman brought something out of the bag as she stood, holding it up for them to see.

Duncan gasped. "What the fuck?"

Phil laughed. "What is that, another Halloween prop?"

Duncan grabbed hold of his friend's arm, gripping it more firmly this time as he again attempted to drag him toward the door. "That's no prop. Come *on*, man. There's something seriously wrong with this bitch."

The woman laughed. "Aw, that hurts my feelings, Dunc."

A sharp coldness penetrated Duncan's still-intensifying weed buzz. Not many people called him Dunc these days, but it'd been his nickname throughout high school, one that held a dual meaning. On the one hand, it was a common way of shortening his name, but in his case, it was also an ironic reference to his lack of prowess on the basketball court.

As in Dunk with a "k", because it was something he couldn't do.

Hearing the masked woman say it now, utilizing that extra, perky emphasis, made that buried memory stir again, but it still wouldn't quite surface. This bothered him immensely and made him try harder to remember.

Jesus, what have I forgotten?

He tugged much harder at Phil's arm. "Come on, goddammit."

The woman was holding up what looked like a severed human head, one freshly removed from the body to which it'd been attached. The ragged neck stump looked like it'd been chopped at multiple times with some razor-sharp implement, an axe or something. That made Duncan think of the clanking sound he'd heard while the woman was rooting around in the bag. The bag didn't look large enough to hold a full-sized axe, but a hatchet or cleaver could definitely be in there, maybe both, along with maybe more tools made for cutting and chopping. The woman's fingers were twined in the dead man's heavily blood-flecked hair. She was swinging the head from side to side, making it look like a grisly pendulum. Blood obscured much of the dead man's face, but after observing it in sick fascination a while longer, he began to perceive something familiar in its contours.

Duncan's breath caught in his throat.

Oh shit. Oh no.

Christopher had shown up for the reunion after all, only no one would get to spend any time rehashing memories of the good old days with him, nor would he ever be able to tell them why he'd done what he'd done twenty-five years ago.

Phil again tore free of Duncan's grasp. "Hold on. Does that look like—"

Before he could complete the thought, the masked woman drew her arm back and slung it forward, sending Christopher's severed head flying toward them. The head's trajectory, intentionally or otherwise, sent it straight at Phil, who wasn't able to flinch out of the way or otherwise react until it hit him in the face. He yelped in pain and took a staggering step backward as the head fell away from him and smacked against the sidewalk at his feet.

The joint Phil had somehow held onto all this time fell from his fingers as his eyes bulged and his breathing started coming in heavier gasps. Tears spilled down his face as he shook his head rapidly in abject denial, his disbelieving gaze riveted to the mutilated body part.

Duncan made one last attempt to muscle Phil away from the gruesome sight and turn him toward the open door, but it was like trying to move a statue. As he did this, the woman again went into a squat and resumed rooting around in her bag.

Though he didn't consider himself a coward, Duncan recognized a lost cause when he saw one. He relinquished his grip on Phil's arm and started toward the door. What he hadn't counted on was the wave of dizziness that came over him with the rapid physical movement. He stumbled forward and bounced off the doorframe instead of passing through the opening. After staggering backward a few steps, he made a slightly more focused attempt to flee into the hallway, but before he could get there, he heard a sound that made him think of silencer sound effects in movies. Heard it several times, in fact. A few times the sound was accompanied by sharp jabs of piercing pain so intense it dropped him to his knees. His eyes filled with tears of anguish at what he thought must have happened. He'd been shot. More than once. Judging from Phil's sudden wail of agony, he'd been shot, too.

A massive wave of terror and distress crashed over Duncan as the full weight of what was happening—of what was *about* to happen—hit him full-force. He was going to die in this lonely little space out behind the gymnasium. The people he loved would never see him alive again. He'd never again hold his wife in his arms. Never see his kids or walk his dog again. All of life's myriad pleasures, great and small, were sliding away from him.

It wasn't fair.

The silencer-like sound came again and he felt another piercing jolt of pain, this time in the region of his shoulder. As the pain throbbed and dispelled his buzz, he looked down and saw the red-covered point of a nail protruding from his shoulder.

He was being shot all right.

But not with a pistol equipped with a long silencer like in the movies. The masked woman was killing him with a nail gun. Even as this realization came to Duncan, he heard the sound of the tool discharging several more nails. A loud thump behind him indicated Phil had hit the ground. Whether he was alive or not, Duncan didn't know, but he wasn't wailing in pain anymore.

Duncan was still on his knees.

He reached for the doorframe with a shaky hand, determined to make one final effort to get up and propel himself through that opening. It was his only hope of survival. Screaming for help was useless. The band in the gym was now playing that godawful Kid Rock song he'd hated back in the day, and he could hear his old classmates rowdily singing along to it at the top of their lungs. A bomb could go off out here and they might not hear it.

Footsteps approached from behind.

Then he felt the woman press the nail gun against the back of his head.

She held it there for several seconds before laughing. "No. I don't think so. That would be a little too merciful."

She kicked him in the back, forcing him to flop forward.

Then she knelt over him and held the nail gun against his back.

"Still don't know who I am, Dunc?"

Duncan sniffled and moaned. "I'm sorry. For whatever I did to you. I'm so sorry."

The woman was silent for a moment.

Then she grunted and said, "Apology not accepted."

She fired a nail into the small of his back.

Duncan's face contorted in even greater agony, and as he attempted to roll over, the woman fired another nail into his back, this time higher up the length of his spine. This was followed by two more nails between the shoulder blades. The multiple perforations of his flesh made him feel like a human pincushion. Instead of relenting at that point, she shifted her position and fired nails into the backs of his knees. By then, he was no longer capable of screaming or calling for help. All he could do was blubber and beg for a quick end to his suffering.

Instead, the masked woman set the nail gun aside and rolled him over.

Then she raised the mask and gave Duncan a long look at her face.

She smiled. "What about now? Still don't remember?"

At first he did not.

But then, all at once, it came to him and everything made sense. The burn scars had faded with time, perhaps with the aid of skin grafts, but enough evidence of disfiguration remained to bring those suppressed memories all the way back to the surface.

"You."

The woman's smile broadened. "Yes, baby. Dear old Dunc. It's

47

me. I pledged my heart to you once, do you remember? Swore my undying love." She shook her head, sighing in a wistful way before her face twisted in an unforgiving sneer of sheer hatred. "But all that was before Chris and I got together, and what you did after that is what really crushed my heart."

She pressed the nail gun against one of his bulging eyes and fired a nail into it. And then another into his other eye. The second of these final two nails entered his head at such an angle that it penetrated his brain and caused his body to seize and twitch for a last few agonizing seconds before going still.

Drayton High's homecoming queen of 1999 pulled the mask back down over her face and retrieved her bag of shiny metallic toys, dropping the nail gun back inside it before taking out the cleaver.

Some more bloody work ensued as she added two more severed heads to her collection. After depositing all three in her bag, she cinched it shut and spent some time dragging the fresh corpses out of sight behind the line of shrubs at the back of the building. She then removed the trash can her latest victims had used to block the door open.

After watching the door swing shut, she draped the bag over her shoulder and started walking fast back the way she'd come.

THREE

THE WHOLE REASON BRIDGETT HOGAN had come to the reunion was to finally see Christopher Schaefer again. She hadn't been to one of these things since the year-five event in 2005 and likely wouldn't have entertained ever attending another one if not for hearing the news about the return of Drayton High's former golden god and prodigal son. Now that it was looking like he might be a no-show, she was contemplating an early departure.

She'd never been close to any of her classmates in the old days. Hers was a curious case in that she wasn't the typical high school loner. She was an attractive girl who received her share of male attention, but she always shunned it, leading most to assume she was into girls instead of boys. It wasn't true, but Bridgett hadn't cared enough to convince anyone otherwise. She was still largely antisocial in the present day, but she'd been especially moody and disaffected back then, genuinely not caring whether anyone liked her or wanted to hang out with her.

The one exception to this rule was Christopher Schaefer.

Everything about him captivated her. She'd felt annoyed with herself at having lustful feelings for someone like him, a conventionally handsome jock with broad shoulders and bulging muscles. This was because she'd long believed she'd take her first lover in college, where she'd be more likely to encounter men more of her type, some skinny poet or sensitive folk musician. The fantasies she started having about Christopher that last year of high school disrupted this notion to a troubling degree. She often tried to stop thinking about him but had little success.

Then one day that year, when she'd been shut away in her bedroom after school, reading a book of the most pretentious sort as usual, she heard the front doorbell ring. Thinking nothing of it, she continued to read until she heard footsteps in the hallway outside her room. Then came a knock on her door. The look on her mother's face when she opened it was unsettling, a mixture of surprise and a barely suppressed excitement. When she said a boy who wanted to see her was at the door, Bridgett was shocked. No boy had come calling at their door since she was a child, when neighborhood brats would knock and ask if she wanted to come outside and play.

She couldn't imagine who it might be.

But of course it was Christopher.

They spent several hours together in her room with the door locked, which from her understanding, was a thing most parents didn't allow their young daughters to do with male visitors. Her parents left her alone with Christopher the entire time, from slightly after four in the afternoon until just after nine that night. Later on when she thought about it, as she often did, it struck her as intensely strange. She never questioned them about it, and the only thing she could ever figure was they hoped the attention of the most popular boy in school—a boy known even to her parents for his gridiron heroics—might turn her into something resembling a normal person after all.

Fat chance of that.

But she did lose her virginity to Christopher that day, at a little over three hours into his five-hour stay in her bedroom. This was after a long period of staring at each other and talking in a stilted, awkward way that eventually loosened up and became more open. She'd never previously interacted with the football player in any direct or intentional way, but he claimed he'd been able to sense her interest in him. He said he thought about her a lot, even going so far as to say he pictured her in his head when he was having sex with his girlfriend. He'd done it so often that he didn't think he could rest until he experienced being with Bridgett for real.

That was all the inducement she needed.

She wanted him anyway, was able to admit that much at last after talking with him so intimately for so long, but it was the naughty factor that sealed the deal. The idea of having sex with another girl's boyfriend excited her, made her feel wicked and wanton. She was surprised by how much she liked that. There was a little bit of the first-time awkwardness right at the start, but she was stunned by how good it ended up being, something she attributed to Christopher being so much more experienced than most boys his age.

Christopher had a friendly conversation with Bridgett's mother in the foyer before he left that night.

He spent the rest of the school year deliberately ignoring Bridgett, even shunning her.

She was heartbroken and reacted by becoming even more withdrawn than usual at school. At home, she spent her time locked in her room and crying into her pillow, caught in the grip of a deep anguish from having been used and toyed with so callously. The feelings were awful, but she felt safe to wallow in them in private. School was another matter. When she was there, she yearned to let out her rage, to have a screaming confrontation with him in the hallway or in the English class that was the only one they had together. Instead, she kept it all tamped down tight, seething inside as she tried hard to ignore being ignored.

Graduation came as such a bittersweet relief.

Upon eventually hearing that Christopher had disappeared, she experienced a resurgence of her anguish, but it was laced with a strong dose of spiteful vindictiveness. She started having fantasies about him again, except now she imagined him dead in a ditch somewhere or stuffed inside some psycho's crawlspace. Her head filled with visions of extreme tortures he endured, and sometimes she masturbated to them, which she knew was deeply strange, but she couldn't help herself.

When she heard he was coming back to Drayton Falls for the reunion, not attending wasn't even an option. She bought a nice new dress and had her hair done. Looking anything less than her absolute best for the long-delayed dramatic confrontation she was planning was unacceptable. If there was any justice in the world, he'd show up looking as bloated and out-of-shape as most of his football buddies. It'd make for quite the contrast, what with her being the same weight she'd been in high school, along with having little visible gray in her hair and few discernible wrinkles.

Now, though, it seemed she was being deprived of her moment of retribution. She stuck around in the gym for a while even after learning of this development, if only because nothing was confirmed. The one-time football star's old buddies were still trying to get in touch with him. In the interest of avenging the heartbreak of the younger Bridgett, she decided to hang in there a little longer.

A point came when she finally wearied of standing apart from everyone else in the gym. Few people had even attempted talking to her, and even those who ventured a few words did so in only the most cursory way, as if they were doing a polite duty before moving on.

Hardly anyone noticed when she slipped out of the gym and embarked on a lonely walk through the school's empty hallways. She was assailed by the expected memories of long-ago days. The ringing of bells between periods, the babble of vapid conversation as students rushed to and fro, the clang of locker doors slamming shut. It was weird how clear the memories were, even with the lockers having all been removed at some point in the intervening years.

From what she understood, the former high school was no longer being utilized in any active fashion by the city. For several years it'd functioned as the miniscule campus of a rinky-dink community college, but now it was nothing but an empty building. There were rumors it might be headed for eventual demolition.

Which would be no great loss.

She turned a corner and continued down another gloomy stretch of hallway, passing by door after closed door, all the windows darkened. The sound of the band rocking out in the gymnasium grew fainter and fainter. It felt a bit like she was leaving one world behind and entering another, more haunted one. Rather than unsettling her, the feeling was something she savored. She began to realize what a foolish, pointless thing coming here had been. What good could be gained from what she'd planned anyway? Even if Christopher showed up, the only lasting wounds she'd inflict were likely to be to her own dignity.

A decision was made.

She would leave now, without returning to the gym or saying even a single word to anyone on the way out, just slink away and return to her quiet and boring adult routine. After a while, she could start pretending she'd never had any real intention of doing anything as ridiculous as what she'd planned. The anticlimax of Christopher's no-show might even allow her to finally put the past to rest forever.

Just as she was turning around to go back the way she'd come, she was stopped in her tracks by a sound emanating from a closed door to her right. Affixed to the door at eye level was a little plaque identifying it as the door to a bathroom, one designated for use by male students.

Bridgett frowned and took a step closer to the door, tilting her head as she strained to hear a repetition of what she thought she'd heard. At first she was sure it must have been an auditory hallucination, one brought on by a collision between her own wandering thoughts and this setting that evoked fevered memories of an unpleasant time in her life. Several silent seconds passed, enough to nearly convince her she hadn't actually heard anything.

She turned away from the door.

And then she heard the sound again.

Her frown deepened because now it was louder and more distinct. This time it repeated almost right away, a shuddering intake of breath followed by what was unmistakably a moan. Not a sound of pain, but of pleasure.

Of sexual excitement.

Bridgett again approached the door.

This time she turned her head and held her breath as she put her ear as close to the wood as she could without touching it. The sound again repeated almost right away. She wondered if someone might be masturbating in there, but then she heard a secondary sound, a groan made by a different person, deeper in timbre. A smirk twitched at a corner of her mouth. A couple was screwing around in there. Whether they were actually fucking, she couldn't tell for sure, but if not, they were definitely doing some stuff that would most likely end up resulting in sex.

That established, her thoughts turned to who she might be hearing. She soon realized she was no longer in any hurry to leave. Listening to the amorous activities of the mystery couple was getting her a little hot and bothered. She pressed a palm flat against the door and felt her breathing quicken as a fantasy formed in her mind, one in which she entered the bathroom and joined the couple for a threesome.

CLASS REUNION SLAUGHTER

A wild scenario for sure but one that would not be without precedent in her life. She'd had a lot of anonymous sex over the years, almost always with people she never saw again. In her younger days during and after college, she'd gone out actively hunting for it all the time. She'd done this in lieu of ever pursuing relationships of any real emotional substance or duration, likely in large part because of lingering trauma from what Christopher had done to her. What she'd learned from that incident was that it was too dangerous to ever let herself feel anything too deeply for anyone. In turn, she'd left her own trail of people with wounded feelings in her wake, but that was their problem, not hers.

It'd been a while, though.

At some vague point a few years back, she'd grown weary of the endless pursuit of anonymous carnal pleasures. In the last year, she'd hooked up with just three men, and the last time had been nearly six full months ago. She was thus strongly tempted to at least attempt to turn this fantasy into reality, despite the unknown variables at play. The people on the other side of this door were almost certainly former classmates, which meant there was a good chance they might be people she loathed. They might be unattractive, perhaps even gross and ugly. If the latter was true, it didn't really matter. She'd apologize for the intrusion and immediately turn around and walk out, leaving whoever it was unaware of what she'd had in mind. On the other hand, if they were people she despised but found desirable ... well, it wouldn't be the first time she'd ever hate-fucked someone.

Far from it.

Sometimes that was the hottest kind of sex of all.

Smiling, she began to push the door open.

It'd only opened a crack when the flat head of a hammer cracked down against the crown of her skull, dropping her to her knees.

Bridgett had no idea what had happened.

The blunt impact had come without warning, with no awareness that someone else had joined her in the hallway, sneaking up from behind while she was preoccupied with her fantasies and the alluring sounds from the bathroom. Even as she swayed on her knees, she still had no concept of any of this. All she knew was she was in pain, a pain so intense it rendered clear thinking impossible.

The hammer came down again and she crumpled to the floor.

The masked woman in the cheerleader outfit stood above her, observing the unmoving form of Bridgett Hogan for several seconds in an impassive way. The unconscious woman was breathing but not moving. She considered taking a moment to finish her off, but of all the people here tonight, Bridgett was the one she least desired to kill. She looked out of commission. Hoping she'd stay that way long enough for her to deal with the human garbage waiting for her in the bathroom, the masked woman stepped over Bridgett and pushed the door open.

FOUR

STACY NELSON HAD NOT COME to the reunion with any serious thoughts of rekindling an adolescent flame or breaking her marriage vows. Though she and Warn Griggs had remained friendly through the years and lived one street over from each other in the same neighborhood, they'd spent those years staying true to their respective spouses. There'd never been any simmering tension between them. High school was the past, a pleasant but distant memory, and they were happy in the separate lives they'd created with their families.

Moreover, they'd each attended all the previous major reunions with no old sparks ever reigniting. Until tonight, they'd never even danced together again since senior prom. On the way to the event, she'd felt no anticipation of things going a different way than usual. As she'd told her husband only a week ago, the last one five years ago was honestly pretty boring. Everyone was getting noticeably older even back then. Fewer people were showing up, either from lack of interest or the usual attrition of death and illness. She'd given serious thought to not going at all, but that changed when she heard the amazing and stunning news about Christopher Schaefer.

Like a lot of other people, she'd long thought Chris was dead, and hearing that he wasn't simultaneously made her deliriously happy and inspired a profound curiosity. She decided there was no way in hell she was passing up what might be her only opportunity to see her old friend again. In the old days, she'd been a vital part of Drayton High's in-crowd and, of course, so was Chris. She'd loved him as much as everyone else had. He was the one guy she'd ever fucked while still in her relationship with Warn. It'd happened only twice and he'd made her swear to keep it secret, something she'd been happy to do because she had no wish to hurt Warn. Plus she knew the score. Chris was just doing what he always did, continuing his never-ending quest to sleep with all the cutest girls.

It was no big deal.

Just like seeing Warn again in the present day was no big deal.

Until she arrived at the reunion, because right away something felt different this time. It wasn't anything she could put her finger on, just something that was in the air, some strange electric charge, a heady feeling that made her feel giddy and alive. She felt a wildness inside her, and along with it came a willingness to let her hair down and flirt with danger just a little bit.

It started with the drinking.

She imbibed considerably more than she had at previous reunions, and by the time the rumors started circulating that Christopher might not show after all, she wasn't as upset about it as she might have been otherwise. Warn peeled away from the group of guy friends he'd spent the first hour drinking with and came over, started chatting her up. They talked for a longer continuous time than they had in many years. The drinks kept flowing. Somewhere along the line they started making eyes at each other the way they had when they were young. Something was happening, that reckless feeling buzzing in her brain again, telling her dangerous things she knew she should ignore.

Then Warn invited her to dance and shortly after that all her remaining inhibitions flew out the window. They danced together for several consecutive songs, getting sweatier and looser with every passing minute, closer and less cautious about staying within the bounds of what was appropriate for two individuals married to other people. The first time she felt his stiffening cock thrust against her ass she knew she'd be breaking twenty years of perfect faithfulness to her husband.

And now here they were in a bathroom together, the farthest one from the gym, where hopefully they could have enough uninterrupted private time together to do that thing they both wanted to do. Stacy knew it was wrong, knew she was being unforgivably bad and breaking sacred bonds, but she didn't care, because it was all coming back to her now, all the old heat and lust. She loved her husband—or at least she thought she did—but never in her life had she been as hot for anyone as she had for Warn when they were young. As they shut themselves in a stall and tore at each other's clothes, it was like the years slipped away. The feeling of Warn's hands gliding over her skin was electric. She moaned at his every touch, growing wetter and desperate with erotic need. She felt consumed with it, as if she'd somehow turned back the clock and actually become young again.

Their clothes on the floor at their feet, she hooked her legs around him and held on for dear life as he entered her and fucked her hard against a side of the stall, grunting and groaning as his length slid in and out of her. Their bodies were sheened with sweat, so much of it they were as slippery as they'd be in a shower. The stall rattled and rattled as Stacy dug her nails into Warn's bare back hard enough to draw blood. In the midst of the frenzy, the wildest thought flitted through her head. She could run away with Warn. They could have this every night and day, as often as they wanted. All their kids were almost grown, so what the hell? Maybe the thought would desert her after the madness of the moment passed, but a part of her thought maybe it wouldn't.

They were so caught up in what they were doing that it took a few moments to realize someone else had entered the bathroom. Warn was still energetically banging her against the side of the stall by the time Stacy's mind belatedly processed the creak of the bathroom's door opening. At least a few seconds had passed since the old hinges produced the sound. Turning her head, she caught a glimpse of someone standing out there, just a sliver through the tiny gap between the stall's frame and the closed door.

The bathroom had three stalls. They were in the middle one. Whoever was out there was standing about five or six feet directly in front of it.

Facing it.

Staring.

Listening.

Stacy felt a stab of fear as some of her wantonness deserted her. She clutched harder against Warn's back and put her mouth against his ear, urgently telling him to stop. Her voice was a fierce whisper at first, which wasn't good enough, because he pounded at her a few more times before she raised her voice and shrieked the word loud enough to get his attention.

He heaved a massive breath as he abruptly stopped thrusting, his sweat-dripping face twisting in confusion. "What is it?"

She nodded toward the door and he finally got it.

His head turned that way and he glowered when he too finally glimpsed the form of the interloper through the crack. "Hey, asshole. Could you maybe stop being such a peeping perv and get the fuck out of here? I mean, what the fuck? All the bathrooms in this place, and you had to come way the fuck out here?"

At first there was no response.

The mystery person stood there and stared.

Then came a metallic clanking sound as something hit the floor. This was followed by a sound of footsteps as the interloper moved away. Stacy felt a flicker of relief, but then the lights went out. She yelped in surprise, but in that moment she felt more anger than fear. A part of her was still afraid but hated that someone out there was fucking with them and ruining this moment. She unhooked her legs from Warn's back and slowly extended them to the floor. Bracing her hands against his chest, she backed him off a step so she could turn fully toward the door.

"Who's out there?" she called out, infusing her voice with as much sneering venom as she could manage. "You better turn those lights on and get lost or I'm coming out there to kill you, I swear to God."

This time there was an audible response.

A girlish giggle.

Then that clanking sound again and this time it was more unnerving. The faint glow of a phone screen was visible through the door gap. It was low to the ground, as if the person using it was kneeling. Stacy recalled the clanking thump of something hitting the floor and wondered what it had been. Her guess was a bag of some sort, one stuffed with a number of items, because it sounded like the woman out there was rooting around in something, banging those metallic objects against each other. She was obviously using the light from her phone to sort through them.

Stacy dropped to her knees and started feeling around on the floor for her purse, finding it at the side of the toilet. Warn asked what she was doing in a hushed voice. She made a shushing sound in reply as she started groping around in the purse, feeling for her phone.

Watching the mystery woman had given her an idea. A part of her wanted to rush straight out there to confront the bitch and put an end to her mind games. She was most likely messing with them out of some twisted idea of fun, but on the off-chance she was up to anything truly sinister, preventative action of some kind seemed warranted. Getting a look at what they were dealing with first seemed like a good idea, though.

Her hand had just closed on her phone when she realized Warn had moved away from her. She heard a sound she recognized as the latch knob turning. He'd unlocked the door and was pulling it open. It seemed he'd had similar notions about confronting the mystery woman, only without exercising the same level of caution.

Stacy turned her head and raised the now glowing screen of her phone to watch him walk through the open door. She glimpsed the faint outline of a dark form kneeling on the floor. Warn was already speaking in a belligerent way, demanding that the stranger vacate the bathroom immediately, though he phrased it in a far more profane way than that. His voice was so loud and so infused with offended rage. She'd never heard Warn sound quite like that. He'd always been such an easygoing guy, never quick to anger, but evidently the stranger's intrusion and subsequent actions had flipped something inside him.

Despite her initial preference for caution, a part of her was glad Warn had acted in such a fearless fashion. She was already starting to relax a little, certain they'd soon have the bathroom to themselves again, perhaps within a few seconds.

This semi-relieved feeling was short-lived. Stacy felt a new flicker of alarm when she saw the mystery woman shift her position on the floor. She yelled at Warn to back off, but it was already too late. The next sound she heard was a high-pitched shriek of searing pain. The kneeling woman had made an upward thrusting motion with her hands, and now she was doing it a second time. Warn shrieked again. Hearing this elicited a terrified scream from Stacy, because even without fully seeing it, she knew what was happening.

She's stabbing him! Killing him!

All she could see clearly was Warn's naked backside as he made a wobbling retreat. He yelped in pain again as his back struck the edge of the stall's frame. Instinct sent Stacy surging to her feet. She reached out and grabbed Warn by an arm and pulled him into the stall, pushing him toward the back as she shut the door and twisted the knob to lock it.

"Listen up, you psycho bitch," she screeched, voice raw and quavery from an overload of fear and anger. "You've still got enough time to fuck off out of here before you end up spending the night in jail, but I'm calling the cops right fucking now."

The mystery woman giggled again.

Warn moaned in absolute misery.

Stacy made her phone's screen light up again and approached him. He was standing with his back against the tiled rear wall, in that narrow space between the toilet and the side of the stall. His shaking hands were cupped over his crotch, hiding the damage the psycho had inflicted, but Stacy could see a trickle of something dark sliding down the hairy inside of his thigh.

Stacy's eyes misted with tears as she gently touched his cupped hands. "Let me see, baby."

He gave his head a fierce shake as tears streamed steadily down his face. "No. No, no, no."

He was blubbering, close to hysterical.

Stacy reckoned she couldn't blame him.

She repeated her previous words and added, "Please, baby. I need to see so I can know how to help you."

His steady whimpering rose in volume, but he at last allowed her to pull his trembling hands away, revealing the damage. Stacy screamed in shock when she saw it, a sound followed by mocking laughter from the woman whose face she still hadn't seen. How anyone could be so deranged—and so cruel—to do what she'd done and then laugh about it was beyond her ability to comprehend.

It was pure evil.

One of Warn's testicles was split open and leaking blood, bisected straight through the middle by a thick blade of devastating sharpness. There was another puncture wound just above the level of his crotch. Now that Warn had pulled his hands away, blood was pouring from both wounds at a steadier rate. The blood brought home the dire level of threat she was facing in a blunter and more emphatic way than anything else had.

If help didn't arrive soon, she was going to die in this bathroom.

Her heart filled with horror and despair at the thought.

It wasn't just that she didn't want to die—which she definitely did not—but the circumstances. She was mortified at the idea of her family learning that she'd died naked in a bathroom while drunkenly hooking up with an old boyfriend. It would forever change how her husband and kids thought of her. This moment of impulsive infidelity would become the defining aspect of her legacy, sweeping all the good things about her aside and leaving only enduring shame in its wake. Everything thrown away just for the sake of a fuck, a few minutes of fleeting pleasure. She thought again of how, in the heat of the moment, she'd briefly entertained the idea of running away with Warn and saw clearly how absurd it was.

All her previous pleasant feelings where Warn was concerned vanished as she watched him tremble and bleed. She feared she was already doomed, but now she wondered, might there still be a way to fight and survive this? Emotion gave way to cold calculation as she took Warn firmly by the wrist and guided him away from the back wall. He came without much resistance, perhaps because he was too distraught and in too much pain to think clearly about what she was doing. She turned him and slipped around behind him.

He gave no indication of realizing she was now using him as a shield. Having a body between her and the crazy woman alone might not save her, but it was better than nothing. Now she needed to call the cops like she'd already threatened and hope like hell they showed up in time to save her. If she survived, she'd likely still face a devastating reckoning with her family, but at least she'd be fucking alive.

She looked at her phone and was right on the precipice of using the voice assistant to call the emergency line when a heavy object came sailing into the stall and struck the wall behind her. The object dropped down and hit the top of the silver plumbing fixture at the back of the toilet before tumbling into the bowl with a splash that sprayed water on her bare legs.

Curiosity caused her to direct the phone's glow at the toilet rather than putting the call through. What she saw floating in the water stunned her into frozen silence for a moment. Then she filled her lungs with air and unleashed the shrillest, loudest scream of her life.

It was Christopher Schaefer's head in the water, his slack features staring up at her like something from a nightmare.

She screamed again.

And then again.

She was so thunderstruck with horror that her brain initially failed to register something of extreme importance, which was that the crazy woman had entered the stall to her left. Boosting herself up by first stepping on the toilet, she grabbed hold of the top edge of the stall's side panel and hauled herself up, hooking a leg over it to hover directly over Stacy, who was still screaming her head off. Once she felt secure enough to maneuver effectively, the woman brought her right arm down in a slashing motion. The edge of the blade in her hand sliced a deep groove down the back of her target's shoulder.

Stacy screamed again, this time in sudden pain.

She wheeled around and raised her phone to aim the light at the masked woman hanging from the top of the stall. The attacker's leering grin was visible through the mouth hole of a black ski mask. Even in the midst of her terror, Stacy's mind registered the oddness of a single detail. The woman's top was instantly recognizable because decades ago she'd often worn one just like it. It was the top piece of a Drayton High cheer outfit. A vintage one, not one of those hideous redesigned modern ones.

The masked woman raised her knife again.

Stacy backed away in time to avoid being slashed a second time.

She again allowed sheer instinct to guide her, sliding past Warn and shoving him toward the back of the stall as she felt for the door knob. Waiting for the cops to swoop in and save her was no longer an option. She couldn't even afford to waste the time it'd take to place the call. Warn cried out in fresh pain as he stumbled and plopped down into the open toilet, resulting in another splash. He called out to her in fear and desperation.

Stacy ignored his pleas as she yanked the door open and raced out of the stall. She knew now her only hope was to move faster than her homicidal adversary and get the hell out of the bathroom before the crazy bitch could take another swipe at her.

Orienting herself in the general direction of the door and the hallway beyond, she took off running. What she failed to account for was the bag the attacker had left on the floor. She tripped over it and went flying, landing hard face-first on the tiles as her phone went skidding away from her. The pain of impact was immense, but the adrenaline pumping through her veins allowed her to push through it. She'd just gotten to her hands and knees in advance of a renewed dash for the door when the woman in the cheerleading outfit kicked her rear end, sending her back to the floor.

The masked woman moved fast, getting around her in time to

deliver a savage kick to the face that loosened some teeth and split her bottom lip. She felt blood in her mouth and spat it out on the floor, then tried rising up again, but she was woozy from the blow to her head and collapsed again. Her assailant moved away and a moment later she heard the flick of a switch.

Old fluorescent bulbs flickered to life overhead, driving away the darkness. Stacy groaned and looked up as the masked woman returned to the area between the stalls and the long ceramic sink basin. She still had the knife. Stacy whimpered at the sight of it. The edge of the shiny serrated blade was wet with fresh blood.

Her blood, commingling with Warn's.

Realizing this had the odd effect of making her more conscious of the throbbing wound inflicted by the blade. Blood was still leaking from the long gash that started at the top of her shoulder and extended several inches down her back. She didn't want to experience that feeling of the blade cutting into her again, parting her flesh with such terrible ease.

The masked woman snatched up the heavy black bag and dumped it on the basin, the objects inside it making that clanking sound again. She put her back to Stacy as she set the knife down and again began rooting around in the bag. The woman's build was slender and athletic, the short cheer skirt showing off legs that were toned and shapely. She was in excellent shape, but there were several telltale indications she wasn't a young girl. Even without seeing her face, Stacy sensed the woman was around her age. Given the setting and context, pegging her as a member of Drayton High's graduating class of 2000 seemed a safe assumption. Stacy was also fairly certain she was someone who hadn't shown her face at the reunion tonight. She would remember seeing another woman who looked this good, as she'd taken significant pride in looking better than just about all her old female classmates.

Gathering her strength, Stacy braced her palms against the floor and rose to her hands and knees. She still felt woozy from being kicked in the head, but she managed to fight off another wave of dizziness as she got shakily to her feet.

The masked woman stopped digging around in the bag and met Stacy's gaze in the long mirror that ran from one end of the basin to the other.

She smiled through the mouth hole. "Hello, Stacy. Long time no see."

Stacy frowned. "You know me?"

The woman laughed. "Of course."

She kept smiling, but did not elaborate.

Stacy glanced toward the door. It was maybe fifteen feet away. She again weighed the pros and cons of making another run for it. Behind her, Warn was still moaning in the stall, weakly muttering her name and begging for help. Hearing his pain stabbed at her heart, but having already made the decision to prioritize her own safety and survival, she shut down the instinctive pangs of empathy. Caring about what happened to Warn would only drag her down. Without realizing it, she'd already started leaning in the direction of the door, the muscles in her body tensing for the dash.

The woman laughed again. "You'll never make it. I'm faster than you. I promise."

Stacy shook her head. "Who are you?"

The woman tilted her head. "You really don't know? My, what short, selective memories you all have."

She pulled up the front of the ski mask to her forehead.

Stacy cringed at the sight of the faded pink burn scars angling across an otherwise pretty face. "You."

The woman pulled the mask back down and nodded. "Yes. Who else would hate you so much? I swear, why are you all so fucking dense?"

Sudden tears spilled from Stacy's eyes. "I'm so ... s-sorry," she said in a warbling voice, surprised by the power of the resurfaced memories, which were accompanied by a long-suppressed sense of shame for the damage done by the act she and her friends had perpetrated. "It was just a stupid p-prank. It ... got out of hand, that's all."

The woman's withering sneer was obvious even through the mask. "Oh, yeah? Just a prank, huh? Well, *this* isn't a fucking prank, bitch."

When she turned around, it was with a hatchet gripped in her right hand. Like the knife, the shiny reflective steel made it look brand new, as if she'd purchased it just earlier today expressly for this occasion.

The woman raised the hatchet as she came a step closer, her deranged smile returning as she said, "Time to cut you down to size."

Stacy screamed and made a break for the door.

True to her word, the woman was faster, moving laterally with shocking speed, getting ahead of Stacy even as she swung the hatchet. The heavy wedge of steel chopped into her side, penetrating three inches deep. Blood gushed from the wound as the masked woman yanked out the head of the hatchet and swiftly brought it around again. This time it punched deep into Stacy's arm, nearly taking it off at the bicep. More blood gushed from the second wound as the attacker again tore the hatchet free.

Stacy staggered backward, away from the door and her only possible route to salvation. Her tears flowed as steadily as the blood pouring from her wounds as she was overcome by the bitter realization that she was doomed. She had no hope of fighting back against this vengeful bitch, especially not in her newly debilitated condition.

Her wounded arm felt like it was hanging by a few thin tendons. It was of no use to her, might as well not even still be there. The pain from these new wounds dwarfed that inflicted by the earlier knife slash. A new wave of lacerating agony accompanied each shuffling backward step. Her knees felt as weak as those of a woman of extreme elderly age, her legs rubbery and almost weightless, on the brink of collapse, yet somehow she remained upright, compelled to continue retreating for as long as she could. She was a slave to the power of that desperate human will to cling to life with everything she had until it was no longer possible.

The attacker smiled as she continued a slow advance, taking one step forward for every backward step Stacy took. "You were the worst of them, you know. Of the girls, I mean. The instigator. The one who laughed the hardest when I begged you not to do it. The one who mocked me and called me a stupid crybaby for filing that police report against Christopher. You remember that, right? The report that was torn up because the town needed their football hero on the field for the big fucking game the next week."

Sniffling, Stacy took another shaky backward step. "I'm sorry. Really, I am. So, so s-sorry." Through her tears, she glimpsed the wide trail of bright red blood she was leaving on the white tiles. It was amazing how much there was. Surely a person couldn't lose that much blood and live for much longer. She might only have a minute or two left. "We were stupid kids. That's all."

The masked woman made a scoffing sound. "Just stupid kids, huh? You ever think about the kid I might have had if Christopher hadn't beaten me into a miscarriage? No, I bet you don't, at least not since back then. You all worked as hard as you could to forget all about that because it would ruin the glorified images you all had of yourselves as members of Christopher's golden inner circle. You convinced yourselves it was all buried forever, that a time would never come when you'd have to pay a price for what you did."

Stacy's retreat came to an end as her back pressed up against the beam separating two of the stalls. She considered shuffling into a stall and locking it, but there was no point. It'd only delay the inevitable by a few seconds.

She shivered in terror but remained where she was as the masked woman drew within striking distance and raised the hatchet. Her bleary gaze went to the shiny head of this instrument of her death, squinting at the way it glinted beneath the fluorescent light. She already knew how it would feel when it came down and slammed into her flesh for a third time, the crushing, blinding agony of it, that deep invasion of heavy steel, an obscene violation, and as she anticipated it, she found a final reserve of spiteful defiance.

This was not the peaceful, far-off end she'd always imagined for herself. She'd taken good care of herself her whole life, living and eating in all the healthiest ways. The road ahead of her should still be long, maybe another forty years or more, with her eventual final days spent in comfort on a cozy bed in her own home and surrounded by family, including grandchildren who hadn't even been born yet.

All that was being taken from her.

Stolen from her.

Her mouth curled in a sneering smile. "Fuck you. You got what you had coming."

The masked woman's mouth dropped open and her eyes bulged.

She screeched in rage.

The hatchet came down.

FIVE

AS CONSCIOUSNESS RETURNED, THE FIRST thing Bridgett Hogan heard was the screaming. The sound was shrill and from somewhere nearby, which was disturbing only in a detached way at first. This was because her most immediate source of concern was the awful pain in her head, which seemed focused at the back of her skull. It felt like she'd been struck with something heavy, maybe more than once, and with enough force to drive her to the floor and render her unconscious.

In those first moments of wakefulness, this was mere guesswork rather than clear memory. She was disoriented, her thoughts out of focus, and had no idea where she was or how she'd come to be in what felt and sounded like a dangerous predicament. The screaming was going on and on, and it clearly was not the sound of a person expressing excitement. It was a sound of desperate terror and pain.

Bridgett grimaced as she opened her eyes and lifted her head off the floor. Hearing that other person's high level of distress cut through the remaining fuzziness clouding her thinking, stirring fresh concerns for her own safety. What she was hearing was what she imagined a person would sound like if they were being savagely murdered. If that was indeed the case, how long would it be before the murderer turned their attention to her?

Another, fainter sound from somewhere farther away further focused her thoughts. She soon realized she was hearing what sounded like a live rock band, which was strange because she hadn't been to any type of music venue in a long time.

Everything came back to her in a flash when she turned her head again and looked up and saw the bathroom door. She gasped as she remembered standing outside the door with her ear pressed to it, listening in a voyeuristic way to sounds of sexual activity that excited her.

She'd been on the verge of pushing the door open when ...

She grimaced again as she at last remembered the heavy blows to the back of her head. An assailant had attacked her in a hallway at her old high school. She was here for a class reunion. The faraway music was from the band playing in the gymnasium. The person who'd assaulted her was now attacking the people she'd heard screwing around on the other side of that door.

Bridgett wasn't sure why the unknown attacker hadn't finished the job on her before moving on to conduct a seemingly far more brutal attack on the amorous couple, though she felt a bitter strain of gratitude for it. She hated that the people being attacked were suffering, but it meant she'd been gifted with a chance to get away and live to see another day.

She groaned through clenched teeth as she struggled to her feet and stood wobbling in the middle of the hallway for a moment. Knowing she didn't have the luxury of waiting for her head to completely clear, she took a tentative first step away from the bathroom. Running away instead of coming to the aid of the person being attacked did make her feel like a bit of a coward, but realistically what could she do? She was a middle-aged woman who'd suffered a head injury, the severity of which was still unknown. The attacker was an armed and violent person apparently intent on committing bloody murder. By attempting to intervene, she'd probably only succeed in getting herself killed, too. The more sensible course of action all around was to head back to the gym as fast as she could and raise the alarm.

Her head was a little clearer now.

CLASS REUNION SLAUGHTER

She took a steadier second step away from the bathroom.

Then she stopped again because she realized there'd been a break in the nonstop screaming, and now she was hearing sounds of conversation from the other side of that door, two women speaking to each other in strident tones. Beneath all this was another sound, a steady background moaning from a third person. The moaning was weak and pitiful, as if the person making the sound had suffered a grievous injury, was maybe on the verge of dying.

Dying, but still clinging to life, albeit perhaps just barely.

The important point was that no one had died in there quite yet.

Also, while the voices from the bathroom were muffled slightly, something about one of them was nagging at her brain, eliciting a distant sense of faint familiarity. The other voice she'd recognized right away. It was Stacy Nelson. She'd overheard the ex-cheerleader talking with some of the other women before commencing her lewd dance floor antics with Warn Griggs. It was Stacy she'd heard screaming in there, which meant it was likely Stacy and Warn were the couple on whom she'd been eavesdropping.

But this other voice ... who was it?

It was the person who'd attacked her, the attempted murderer, undoubtedly, but why did she feel like it was someone she either knew or had known long ago?

Bridgett turned toward the door and began a slow approach. She'd started doing this prior to making any conscious decision to do so, driven by a deepening curiosity. Despite the danger, it felt important to know who this other person was. At the same time, another part of her brain was warning against it, urging her to turn around and run for help as she'd originally planned.

For the second time that night, she put her ear to the door and listened, straining to hear every word.

Within less than a minute, she knew who the other person was.

She pushed the door open and entered the bathroom.

SIX

BEFORE THE MASKED WOMAN COULD bury the hatchet blade in her flesh, Stacy was shoved out of the way from behind by Warn Griggs, who'd summoned some final bit of strength in time to heave himself out of the toilet and come to her rescue. In the process of doing this, he put himself in the path of the descending blade, which chopped down into his skull, the steel penetrating inches deep just above the level of his forehead.

Stacy saw all this happen in the mirror above the basin. The hard shove from Warn had propelled her toward it. She collided with the basin's edge and had to grab onto the faucet of the nearest sink to keep from tumbling to the floor, which would have spelled certain doom. Still staring at the mirror, she saw the assailant attempt without success to wrench the hatchet out of Warn's skull. To her amazement, the horrendous wound did not kill him instantaneously. He groaned incomprehensibly as he wrenched his head around, causing the assailant to lose her grip on the hatchet's rubber handle. Staggering away from her, he wobbled about for a moment like a movie zombie, ambulating with an awkward clumsiness so unlike how he'd always been. It was hard to believe this was the same man who'd danced with her with such athletic abandon a short while ago.

The masked woman was laughing at him, a sound that got louder as he finally collapsed to the floor.

Stacy's eyes flicked to the knife the woman had left on the basin. She seized it in her right hand, the only one she could still use, and spun about, launching herself in the direction of the masked maniac, her useless, nearly severed left arm flopping about like the arm of a rag doll. As she did this, she caught a fleeting glimpse of a new presence in the bathroom at the edge of her peripheral vision. A hopeful thought flashed through her brain, that perhaps help had finally arrived.

"Watch out!"

That was the new arrival, calling out a warning to the masked woman. So much for the cavalry coming to the rescue. On the plus side, the warning did not come in time to allow Warn's killer to fully dodge the blade. The masked woman did twist far enough aside to elude a mortal wound, but the knife sliced deep as it tore open the front of the old cheerleading top and cut a long, bloody line across her abdomen. The assailant screeched in pain and leapt backward as Stacy spun around and took another swipe at her. This time the knife sliced only through open air.

Stacy turned toward the basin and saw the masked woman reach into her overstuffed black bag again. Soon she would have another weapon in hand. Any hope of survival depended on killing her now. The woman's back was to her. She wouldn't get another chance as good as this one.

As she tensed to take another run at the killer, she glanced at the new arrival in the bathroom, scowling the instant she recognized Bridgett Hogan. She'd seen Bridgett in the gym earlier but hadn't given her a second thought, ignoring her just as she had back in their high school days. She'd shared a catty laugh with some of the other ladies over the absurdity of Bridgett showing up for the reunion. The loser bitch had no business being here. No one had ever liked her because of how weirdly aloof she'd always been, as if she thought she was better than the rest of them, despite being a total nothing dud of a person. It figured a bitch like that was siding with the killer.

For all Stacy knew, they were working together.

There was no way to know and it was something she could worry

BRYAN SMITH

about if she survived beyond the next few seconds. She gripped the
knife tighter and started across the floor, moving fast, her attention
fully on the masked woman's back. This time she wouldn't just graze
the bitch. Her plan was to ram the big blade into her body all the way
up to the hilt, then yank it out and do it again.

And then again.

As many times as it took to send the murdering bitch to hell.

The next thing Stacy knew she was airborne, her bare feet having
slipped in the blood covering a wide swath of the floor tiles. She
crashed onto her back, the knife flying out of her hand. The nearly
severed lower part of her left arm flopped over and smacked her
across the face.

Sitting up, she looked toward the basin and saw that the masked
woman had turned around and was now aiming something at her that
looked vaguely like a gun. Or maybe some kind of power tool.

Stacy whimpered, shaking her head. "Don't ... please ..."

The masked woman's only answer was a click of a button.

73

SEVEN

BRIDGETT WINCED WHEN THE NAIL gun sent a high-speed sliver of steel flying into Stacy Nelson's open mouth. She gasped in horror as three more nails were dispatched in rapid succession. One went into Stacy's throat. The final two struck her in the face, one penetrated an eye, while the final one punched dead-center into her forehead. Stacy crumpled weakly to the floor and twitched a few times before going still.

The masked woman turned toward Bridgett, aiming the nail gun at her midsection. Instead of immediately filling her body with nails, the woman sighed and shook her head. "You should have stayed where you were, feigned unconsciousness or whatever. I've got nothing against you, Bridgett. I probably would have left you alone after dealing with these assholes."

Overwhelmed by sheer terror, Bridgett nonetheless strove for a steady, calm tone as she said, "You could still do that. I'm no threat to you."

The woman grunted. "But you know who I am, don't you?" She

raised the nail gun, aiming it at Bridgett's face. "Am I wrong?"

Bridgett felt on the brink of collapse, her terror was so great.

Her mouth opened and her jaw muscles worked as she tried to say something, but the lump that formed in her throat made pushing the words out difficult.

The woman pulled up the front of the ski mask. "Say my name. Show me that you remember. Show me that you're not like the rest of them."

Bridgett swallowed thickly and cleared her throat. "Of course I remember you, Angela. You were the only person in high school who was ever nice to me."

Angela Conroy pulled the ski mask the rest of the way off and tossed it onto the basin. She fluffed out her long blonde hair with her free hand while keeping the nail gun trained on Bridgett. It was amazing how good she still looked despite the thin burn scars arcing diagonally across her face.

Her smile had a distinct tinge of sadness. "Yes, I was nice to you, but only after a certain point. For the longest time, I was just as mean to you as the rest of them. Do you want to know why that changed?"

Bridgett shrugged. "I always figured it had something to do with Chris."

Angela nodded. "Of course it did. He told me, you know, about what he did to you. How he manipulated you into letting him fuck you with your parents listening down the hallway. He thought that was so funny. I wish I could say I was better than that, but I wasn't, not back then. I laughed, too. I was just like them, cruel and thoughtless, until Chris got me pregnant."

Bridgett recalled how for one tumultuous week in the fall of 1999 whispers of Chris assaulting the homecoming queen ran rampant in the halls of Drayton High. The word going around was that what he'd done was so bad he was in danger of being expelled, that he might even go to jail for a long time.

Then, like magic, the charges against Chris were dropped and everything went back to normal.

Seemingly normal, that is.

Angela dropped out of sight for a while and didn't return until after Christmas break, with bright pink burn scars on her face. No official story ever circulated about that, but of course there were more whispered rumors.

"They made me out to be a liar, a dirty little jealous whore making up stories for attention." She huffed bitter laughter. "Then I got lured over to Warn's place one weekend when his parents were out of town. They were all there. Phil and Dunc. Some of the other football players. Stacy and about half the fucking cheer squad. They told me they wanted to have a serious talk about Chris, how he was out of control and something needed to be done. I should have known something was off when I showed up and they had the grill going. A lot of them helped hold me down, but it was Stacy who pressed my fucking face into that hot steel." She directed a quick, sneering glance at the naked dead woman on the bloody floor. "Judge me all you want, but I don't regret anything I've done tonight."

Bridgett shuddered, nodding. "I'm not judging you. Truly, I'm not. These people did you wrong. I understand your rage. But you've taken your revenge. Maybe it's time to let it go now. Put the past to rest."

Angela laughed. "Do you honestly expect me do that at this point?" She shook her head. "No, it's too late for that. Besides, you're wrong. My revenge is not yet complete."

Bridgett frowned. "But haven't you heard? Chris isn't coming. He's a no-show."

Angela's laughter was louder this time, almost jovial. "That's where you're wrong. He's a so-called no-show because I killed him in the parking lot." She indicated the row of stalls with a lift of her chin. "His head's floating in the toilet in there. Take a look if you don't believe me."

Bridgett's trembling worsened as she shook her head. "That's okay, I believe you. But if you've already killed Chris, what's left?"

Angela sneered and took a sudden step closer, startling Bridgett. "It's not done until they're *all* dead. The entire fucking Drayton High class of 2000."

Bridgett flinched at the sudden movement and took a corresponding backward step. "But there's over a hundred of them here tonight. You can't possibly hack and chop your way through all of them."

Angela pursed her lips and made a thoughtful sound as she appeared to give the matter some consideration. "You're probably right about that." Her lips stretched in a deranged grin. "Which is why I planted bombs in the gym. Speaking of which …" She glanced at a watch strapped to her left wrist. "Hmm, yes, they'll be going off in less than three minutes."

Bridgett's mouth dropped open in a look of disbelieving horror.

Then she said, "But ... you're talking about a slaughter. A mass fucking slaughter."

Angela nodded. "Yes. And you're the only one who knows who planned it. Like I said, you should have stayed where you were. This far from the gym, you might even have survived the explosion."

There was a click and an instant later a nail drilled into Bridgett's shoulder, the pain propelling her backward. Her back slammed into the section of wall next to the door. She spun away in time to avoid being perforated by another nail, getting a hand on the door handle as she heard the nail plink against the tiled wall. As Bridgett pulled the door open, Angela shifted her aim and sent more nails in her direction. Because Bridgett was already moving through the doorway, most of them missed, but one hit her in the shoulder inches from where the first had penetrated. The pain was incredible, but she didn't let it slow her down as she started racing down the hallway at the fastest speed she could manage. Luckily for her, she could move at a pretty good clip when sufficiently motivated.

She heard more clicking and plinking sounds as Angela followed her into the hallway and continued firing the nail gun. Instead of moving in a straight line, Bridgett weaved and zagged. The evasive running pattern was effective at helping her avoid being struck again. For the most part. It also helped that a nail gun, used as a weapon, wasn't as accurate as a firearm from any significant distance. These things didn't mean she could afford to let up, though. Angela was charging after her at a pace that nearly matched her own, firing again and again as she gained speed, screaming in rage the whole time. Bridgett's lungs and leg muscles strained uncomfortably as they were pushed to their absolute limit.

At one point, sensing that Angela was getting closer, she risked a glance over her shoulder, and that was when another nail finally found flesh. This one hit the point of her right elbow. It failed to penetrate deeply and fell out after she'd taken a few more long strides. That was fortunate, but the impact sent a sting of pain down the length of her arm that hurt like a bastard. This was bad, but the truly alarming thing was that Angela did appear to have closed the gap between them by at least a few feet, thanks in part to wearing sneakers as opposed to the pumps Bridgett had selected as her footwear for the night. She wished she'd made another choice, but then again, she hadn't expected to end the night by running for her life. At least she wasn't in high fucking heels.

CLASS REUNION SLAUGHTER

The clicking sound to her rear continued, but Bridgett soon realized she was no longer hearing the plinking of nails striking walls or hitting the floor. A screech of even louder rage from Angela seemed to confirm what she suspected, that the power tool's supply of nails was already depleted. Bridgett experienced a moment of ecstatic relief until something heavy hit the center of her back, staggering her badly enough to send her careening into the wall to her left. She bounced off it and staggered back into the middle of the hallway.

Through some miracle, she managed to stay upright and continued moving forward, but the impact of whatever it was—probably the nail gun itself—slowed her enough that Angela was finally able to catch up to her. She crashed into Bridgett from behind, landing atop her as she drove her to the floor.

Trapped beneath the murderous former cheerleader, Bridgett tried her best to fight back and squirm her way out from under the other woman, but Angela had all the leverage. Straddling Bridgett's back, she seized a handful of her hair and started slamming her face into the floor, all the while screaming more shrilly than ever. Multiple teeth chipped and broke in Bridgett's mouth as the assault continued. Her strength felt like it was draining little by little, diminishing each time her face struck the hard floor tiles.

Also starting to fade was her will to fight. She wanted to tap some deep reserve of inner power and womanly warrior spirit, to call upon the indomitable will of ancient immigrant ancestors, but in this regard desire alone proved woefully insufficient. There was nothing she could do. She was as stuck as an insect caught in the middle of a spider's web.

Angela got to her feet and placed the sole of a sneakered foot against the back of Bridgett's neck. "As fun as this has been, I'm afraid I have to be going. A part of me really does hate that I have to do this."

The pressure on her neck lifted for a moment.

Bridgett's eyes widened as it hit her what was about to happen. The psycho bitch was preparing to stomp down on her neck in an effort to break it. The sudden insight gave her a fraction of a second to act and she didn't waste it, calling on all her remaining strength to roll fast out of the way. An instant later, as Angela's foot came down and struck only the floor, Bridgett swept her legs around and took Angela's legs out from under her. The crazy woman yelped as she pitched backward, landing hard on her ass as Bridgett got to her feet and resumed her interrupted flight down the hallway.

She turned a corner at a hallway junction and entered the long stretch that would lead back to the gym. About a third of the way down, she risked another backward glance, certain she would again see Angela hot on her heels, but there was no sign of her. Given what she'd said about the bombs, it seemed probable she'd broken off the chase and was in the process of leaving the building through an alternate exit.

Once again, she was faced with the dilemma of whether she should act to save herself or attempt to intervene on behalf of people who, even all these years later, didn't give one shit about her. She was the same nothing she'd always been, a non-entity as far as they were concerned.

She slowed her pace slightly as she continued down the hallway, no longer running all-out as she fretted over the matter. These people didn't like her. They weren't her friends. That wouldn't change even if she successfully played the part of savior tonight. Would anyone even believe her if she charged in there and screamed "*Bomb!*" at the top of her lungs? Hell, would they even hear her over the music? Even if she could get their attention and convince them of the severity of the threat, how long would it take to herd them all out of the building?

Too long.

Her jogging pace slowed to a fast walk.

She considered turning around and seeking an alternate exit of her own. Not just because of her enduring antipathy toward all her former classmates, but also because the situation felt hopeless. This was the inescapable conclusion she'd come to after weighing all the variables. She was certain she was now too late to save anybody. The attempt was the right and humane thing to do despite all her misgivings. She knew that. It was just no longer possible. So much time had already passed, factoring in the chase through the hallway and subsequent struggle. What was it Angela had said back there in the bathroom?

That the bombs should be going off in less than three minutes?

Hadn't it already been longer than that?

Bridgett believed so.

Significantly longer, in fact.

She felt her chest loosen as new hope bloomed inside her. Maybe the bombs were duds. Angela was a former cheerleader and homecoming queen. She'd been through a lot, yes, and was clearly an evil and deranged person, but how much of a munitions expert could she really be? It was, of course, possible for unhinged people to research and learn how to build such devices, but the odds of something going amiss where home-brewed explosives were concerned struck her as quite high.

She was still thinking about this when another abrupt realization came to her, one that caused her to stop in her tracks for a moment and listen. After standing absolutely still for a longish stretch of seconds, she let out a breath and shuddered, not knowing whether to feel relieved or even more worried.

The band had stopped playing.

In fact, she heard no sounds at all issuing from the gym, which was now less than a hundred feet away. The total silence endured as she continued in that direction, walking slowly now, dread building inside her. She wanted to believe the bombs had been discovered and neutralized somehow, or that everyone had evacuated the building after the discovery. That would simplify things in a wonderful way, take this terrible burden she did not want off her shoulders.

So much more time passed as she neared the end of the slow final stretch of her journey through the hallway. At the end, her mind circled back to the conclusion she hoped was true. The bombs were either duds or they'd been disarmed.

What other options could there be?

She found out when she arrived at the open doors to the gym and peered inside.

Bridgett gasped in shock and put a hand to her mouth.

Oh no …

No bombs had gone off, but there were bodies everywhere, splayed all over the floor around the refreshments tables and the dance area in front of the stage. More bodies were slumped down in chairs or tangled together on the floor in front of the open bar. Many of the dead looked as if they'd tried to grab onto each other, either in helpless desperation to save themselves or doomed attempts to help others stricken by whatever had happened here.

Of the band, there was no trace.

Their instruments and gear were gone, and there were no bodies on the stage.

There was no question everyone else was dead. No one was twitching or struggling to breathe. Whatever mass struggle had occurred here was over. In addition to the titanic sense of horror engulfing her, Bridgett was stunned that all this had happened in the time since she'd left the gym, which didn't seem all that long ago. Counting her period of unconsciousness, she couldn't imagine that more than thirty minutes had passed and even that seemed a stretch.

Whatever the case, the evidence of her senses was undeniable.

There was no one to save here.

Bridgett turned away from the grim spectacle of mass death and retraced her tracks back to the bathroom where Stacy and Warn had been killed. She'd dropped her purse back there and needed to retrieve it. Once she'd done that—while averting her eyes from all the blood and the mutilated corpses—she hurried out of the old school and made her way across the parking lot to her Chevy Bolt.

A fluttering scrap of paper was clipped to her windshield wiper. She snatched it free and read the note scrawled across it.

No bombs. My idea of a joke. Ha-ha. Lots of poison, though. Did you like my boyfriend's band? They did such a KILLER job, don't you think? HA-HA. HAHAHAHAHA.

No signature, but did it really need one?

Bridgett crumpled the note and shoved it into her purse.

After she was safely ensconced behind the wheel, Bridgett stared toward the entrance of the building, melancholy tinging her thoughts as memories of the countless times she'd walked through those doors decades ago taunted her. They were not warm and nostalgic thoughts, but there was an underlying wistfulness, a wish to be young again and have a chance to be a better version of herself, one that didn't end up alone as an adult with zero close friends.

She also gave some thought about how to proceed.

Calling the police was the obvious thing to do. The *right* thing.

But she was the sole survivor here, and as such, she would end up spending endless hours being interrogated during the investigation. With so many dead, it'd be a big story, probably even on a national level. Did she want to be at the center of that kind of unrelenting attention?

She shuddered at the thought.

Just get out of here and get home, worry about it later. The note will prove you had nothing to do with this.

Bridgett started her car.

She was reaching for the gearshift when Angela Conroy sat up in the back seat.

LUST FROM BEYOND THE STARS

THE THING ABOUT "FAT" BOB Abernathy was that even two years and counting since he'd shed most of the excess weight that had earned him the nickname, most people in Drayton Falls still called him Fat Bob. His daddy always said people in the town were too stuck in their ways, that once they got used to a thing being a certain way, they would forever have a hard time wrapping their heads around that thing becoming some other kind of way.

A lot of people would have some hard feelings over a thing like that, maybe even develop a life-damaging complex about it.

But not our Bob.

He's a good-natured guy. A bit wild and troubled in some ways, but few people in Drayton Falls dislike him. He's had some hard times, including some severe mental health struggles, but despite all that, he retains his outwardly sunny disposition. Even most of the kids who used to pick on him in middle school eventually became his friends or at the very least stopped being actively mean to him.

One other thing about Bob.

The boy is a teller of tall tales.

Outrageous stories ranging in subject matter from the wildly un-likely to the flat-out impossible in any true real-life scenario. Among other things, he claims to have had no less than six up-close encounters with Bigfoot. Eyes roll a lot when Bob goes into one of his stories, but people listen anyway because they always find them entertaining, even when he's serving up a heaping pile of the most ridiculous steaming horseshit you've ever heard.

Here's the thing, though.

Even though somewhere around 98.7% of Fat Bob's stories are made-up poppycock fueled by untold gallons of cheap beer and prime ganja, every once in a blue moon one of them is true. In fact, one of the most outlandish and unbelievable of all his tall tales is the straight-up, honest-to-God, unembellished absolute truth.

This is that story.

~

Fat Bob wished the driver of the shitty old Isuzu idling in front of him would make up his damn mind already. The goddamn son of a bitch was still hemming and hawing after at least five minutes of staring at the drive-thru menu boards and jawing with the distorted voice emanating from the speaker pole out back of Big Fiesta Burgers.

Dude couldn't decide whether he was in the mood for a box of classic sliders or some of the zesty tacos the joint had recently added to its array of fine culinary offerings. He was being more wishy-washy about it than a Washington politician. Where was Lee Harvey Oswald when you needed the motherfucker?

Bob was significantly slower to anger than the average person. In most such situations, the indecisiveness of the person ahead of him wouldn't ruffle his feathers much, but on this occasion he was feeling a touch more impatient than his norm.

Bob was eager to be done with his business here and get on over to the hootenanny at the rundown old farm Walt Dickens had inherited from his grandpa a few years back. Walt wasn't much for tending the land in the manner of a traditional farmer, but one thing he knew how to do very well was throw a big ole blowout of a backwoods party. Half the folks in this part of Drayton Falls showed up every time he hosted one of his shindigs. There was dancing, music, and fireworks, plus a veritable plethora of fine-looking ladies in immodest attire.

One lady in particular he was looking forward to seeing at Walt's this evening was a fine little number named Bonnie Grace. Her full name was Bonnie Grace Harper, but her first and middle names were always used in conjunction.

Just last night Bob had bumped into Bonnie Grace at the Circle

K gas station over by the Starry Skies trailer park. She was her usual bubbly self as they had a friendly interaction. Her parting words to him as she walked out of the Circle K was that she hoped to see him at the hootenanny.

And that wasn't all.

Before she walked out the door, she winked at him.

Bob had added a pack of Trojans to his purchases.

Just in case.

What all that meant now, as he stewed behind the wheel of his ancient 1985 Honda Civic, was he'd had about enough of listening to the droning fool in the Isuzu, who was still going on and on. Bob became fed up, leaning out his open window to yell at the guy.

Isuzu Guy's only response was a raised middle finger.

He then went back to staring slack-jawed at the menu.

A corner of Bob's mouth curled in a quivering, Elvis-like sneer. His brow furrowed and his eyebrows began to twitch. A tiny flicker of something like genuine anger intruded on his faltering good mood.

His head swiveled slowly to the right.

"I realize it's against the terms of my release from the loony bin, but I do believe I might have to get up out of this motherfucker and administer a beating of such savage severity they'll speak of it with awe for generations to come. It will become a cautionary tale mean-spirited mothers tell their small children at bedtime." He adopted a voice that was a fair approximation of an admonishing mother. "Be good, little ones, or Fat Bob's fist of doom will descend upon you."

Zeke "The Freak" von Rothenberger cackled and slapped one leather-clad thigh, shaking long blond curls out of his face. "That's the spirit, bro. Get out there and teach that fool a lesson about who not to be messin' with." He made devil horns of his fists and shook them like he was at a metal show. "Lay a beatdown on that ass-clown and send him back to Lame Town. Yowzer!"

His subsequent loud whoop of enthusiasm made him sound like the frontman of an '80s metal band hyping up an arena crowd between headbanging anthems. The demeanor meshed perfectly with his attire and appearance. Clad only in assless leather chaps, snakeskin cowboy boots, and tattoos, Bob's passenger-seat companion had bright yellow blond hair that hung well past his shoulders. He had skull rings on his fingers and a multitude of clanking metal bracelets on each wrist. Dark sunglasses hid eyes the shade of a bright blue summer sky. All in all, he looked exactly as if he'd stepped out of an

OUT COME THE FREAKS

MTV *Headbanger's Ball* video from 1989.

Which was no coincidence.

Zeke wasn't real, at least not in the flesh and blood way. He was the imaginary friend Bob's fragile psyche had conjured up during his childhood, back during that phase when he'd spent maybe too much time watching his dad's old VHS tapes, including, yes, several episodes of the aforementioned video compilation show.

This was the first time Zeke had popped up in quite a while, having largely been medicated out of existence in the aftermath of Bob's release from the mental hospital. On the rare occasions when he did materialize these days, it was almost always a sign of psychological disturbance.

Bob frowned, gripping the steering wheel harder as he tried desperately to calm his fraying nerves. "I don't know, man. Things have been good for a while now. I'd hate to get out of hand and end up back at that place."

That place being, of course, the mental hospital.

Zeke brayed another round of wild laughter, after which he took a huge swig from a big bottle of Jack Daniel's that had not been there moments ago. His illusory intrusions into Bob's reality were often like that, developing to include extra little details after he showed up. Sometimes, like now, it was a bottle of whiskey, always Jack Daniel's, an essential '80s rocker accessory required by unwritten law. Other times he had new piercings or fresh ink. One memorable time he'd shown up with a couple of big-breasted blonde groupies with mile-high '80s hair, along with a pungent scent of cheap hair spray that hung over them all like a toxic cloud.

Bob knew this was all the work of his imagination. What was weird about it was how he was never consciously aware of his brain's illusion-building machinations. In this case, just for instance, he didn't look at Zeke and think, *He should have a bottle of Jack.*

It was just suddenly there, like Zeke himself.

Bob's brain was a weird place.

Zeke smirked and tugged his sunglasses far enough down the bridge of his nose to afford Bob a glimpse of his twinkling blue eyes. "Brace yourself, son, because I'm about to lay some heavy shit on your formerly wide ass. You can't let fear hold you back. Being afraid is for chump-ass motherfuckers, and you, my friend, are *not* a chump-ass motherfucker. Are you?"

Bob's frown deepened. "Um ..."

88

In truth, he was spectacularly unsure on this count.

Zeke shook his head, swirling his wild mane of curly blond locks. "Dude, I'm disappointed in you. You've got a hot date with a smokin' hot babe, but right now you're being cockblocked by the universe, which has placed this obstacle in front of you. It's a test of your mettle, of your worth as a man. So my question to you is ... can you pass the fuckin' test, bro?"

Bob began to nod. "Yes, I think so."

"*Hell yeah!*"

That was Zeke unleashing his arena-shaking rock god Thunder Voice again.

Bob put the Civic in park and reached for the door handle.

Before he could pop the door open, the Isuzu at last began to roll away from the speaker pole. The instant this happened, Bob felt the anger rapidly leave his body, like air escaping from the pinched end of a balloon after release. He sighed as he leaned back in his seat, overcome with relief. Though he was far from incapable of violence if pushed far enough beyond his usual limits, it was so antithetical to his normal mode of existence he always felt at least mildly nauseated in the aftermath of any such incidents.

He chuckled ruefully, shaking his head. "Oh man, I am so happy I didn't have to whoop that ass-dragging knucklehead's narrow ass. Would've put a real bummer of a spin on such a nice day. You know what I mean?"

A few seconds ticked by with no response.

Zeke was gone. The passenger seat was empty.

Bob wasn't surprised. In years past, when Zeke had popped in on a more frequent basis, this was how it'd always gone when the stress factors precipitating his appearances were removed or alleviated.

Bob worked the Civic's gearshift and eased the car forward, passing the speaker pole without a glance at the menu. He sat idling behind the Isuzu another few minutes as the driver had a testy exchange with the employee at the drive-thru window. The driver made a slow and halting inquiry about some of the items in his large order. The exchange was civil at first, but the employee soon became agitated, her voice inflected with scathing venom as it rose to a higher and higher register.

A big grin formed on Bob's face as he listened to some of the colorful language that spewed forth in rapid-fire fashion from the young lady's creatively profane mouth. She'd evidently put up with all the nonsense she was willing to take from Isuzu Guy. Judging from the man's shellshocked expression, he was on the verge of crying. The employee leaned out the window and pushed multiple food bags into his shaking hands. She then threw a pile of crumpled napkins at him, some of which hit him in the face, while others fluttered to the ground. When she threatened to empty his cranium with a shotgun shell if he didn't get the fuck gone, he hit the gas and burned rubber out of the parking lot.

Bob was still chuckling as he pulled up to the drive-thru window. "Hey, Kelsey. Dave in there?"

Kelsey Robbins's face was still locked in an agitated sneer. "What the fuck, Fat Bob. You didn't order anything."

His grin took on a sheepish aspect. "Yeah, sorry, I ain't hungry. Just wanted to check in and see if you guys might be headed out to Walt's hootenanny tonight. Gonna be a big ole time."

Kelsey's face registered disbelief. "Goddamn, Fat Bob. You mean to tell me you came through the motherfuckin' drive-thru and waited all that time behind that festering pile of donkey dung masquerading as a human being when you could have just come inside, asked your fucking question, and already been on your goddamn way?"

Bob couldn't help wincing a little. "Yeah, I guess that *was* pretty dumb, huh?"

Kelsey rolled her eyes, adopting a faux-stupid tone as she said, "Ya think?"

Bob tapped the rim of his steering wheel with his thumbs. "So, um … could I talk to Dave?"

Kelsey smirked. "He's in the shitter. Wolfed down too many of our new zesty tacos on break. Gonna be blowin' smoke out of his asshole for a while, most likely."

Bob frowned. "Hmm. I see."

Kelsey sighed. "You don't need to talk to him anyway, bitch. Much as I'd love to throw down at Walt's, we'll be here all night."

"Thought you guys never did the overnights anymore."

Kelsey shook her head in disgust. "Mostly we don't, but the whole rest of the crew quit on us again today. I'd just shut the place down after midnight and go, but Mr. Conroy was none too happy the last time we pulled that stunt."

Bob nodded. "I see. Well, that sucks."

Kelsey grunted. "That it does. Get the fuck out of here. We're off tomorrow. Come hang at our place and get fuckin' wasted with us then. But tonight we're stuck here and there ain't nothin' we can do about it."

Bob sighed in resignation. "Sorry to hear it. See y'all tomorrow. Love ya, Kels."

She snorted, a hint of a smile playing at the edges of her mouth. "Love ya, Fat Bob. Now move on, bitch. You're holding up the line."

Bob resisted sneaking a peek at his rearview mirror, knowing already no other vehicles were waiting behind him. He drove away from the open drive-thru window, never noticing as the silent alien spacecraft hovering over the roof of Big Fiesta Burgers rose higher into the sky and trailed after him, tracking his progress as he turned onto a two-lane backroad and headed out to Walt Dickens's place.

~

Around ten minutes later, after cautiously guiding the rickety old Civic down the bumpy and narrow private drive leading to Walt's derelict farm, Bob arrived at the hootenanny. Though it was early in the evening, with only faint traces of dying daylight still visible at the edge of the horizon, the event was already in full swing. As he swung his vehicle in the direction of a large open area that once upon a time was a cornfield, Bob caught a tantalizing whiff of sizzling meat through his open windows.

Back there at Big Fiesta Burgers, he hadn't thought he was hungry, but now his stomach rumbled at the mouthwatering smells. Perhaps he'd help himself to a juicy chunk of roasted pig while waiting for Bonnie Grace to arrive, along with a big cup or two of beer from the multiple kegs that were no doubt already in place and pumping out gallons of that foamy goodness. He'd have to carefully regulate his beer intake and not get carried away, though. Bob loved beer more than most things, but too much too soon was likely to hamper his chances of getting anywhere fun with the current object of his deep desire. He was good to go with a lady on a sexual level after up to six or seven beers, but beyond that, the functionality of his equipment became iffy at best.

As per usual when Walt hosted one of these big throwdowns, the ex-cornfield functioned as a makeshift parking lot. Already dozens of cars and trucks were spread out all over the place. Bob found a spot near a beat-up GTO and parked there, recognizing it as belonging to his pal Herk Loomer.

After shutting off the Civic's engine, Bob leaned over and opened his glovebox, drawing out the strip of Trojans he'd bought at the

Circle K. He tore off three and shoved the rest back in the glovebox, snapping it shut again. Three Trojans was likely at least two more than he'd actually need, but in matters of amour, Bob was like a boy scout—he believed in being prepared.

He got out of the Honda and threw the door shut without bothering to lock it. There was nothing worth stealing in the old rust bucket, except maybe the rest of the Trojans, and if somebody swiped those and used them to have casual sex the responsible way, more power to them.

The thought brought a grin to Bob's face as he approached the large open area between the ramshackle old farmhouse and the broken-down old barn behind it. The odor of roast pig turning on a spit above a crackling fire got stronger with every step he took. His stomach rumbled as his hunger again made its presence known, producing a sound almost like a belch.

Bob spied some good old boys he recognized clustered around two grills at the back of the farmhouse. They were the same guys who always manned the grills at Walt's parties. For hours, they'd keep a steady supply of fresh burgers and dogs coming, only stopping after they got so drunk they started burning everything to a crisp.

More food was arrayed across two long, cloth-covered tables, including all the cookout basics of barbecue, spare ribs, and much more. On more than one occasion at these things, Bob had gorged himself to the point of being physically ill, but that was mostly back in the days when he'd been Fat Bob for real instead of Fat Bob in name only. He didn't ever want to go back to being that old version of himself, but lord how all those heady aromas tempted him.

As he drew closer to the center of it all, a bunch of people raised their beer cups in salute and called out his name. It was like walking into an outdoors version of the bar on *Cheers*. Herk spotted him almost right away and brought over a freshly poured cup of Bud. Bob accepted it and took a few sociable sips as he made small talk with his friend while surreptitiously casting his gaze around in search of Bonnie Grace.

It wasn't long before he spotted her walking alone out of the barn. A smile lifted the corners of his mouth. He was just about to excuse himself and mosey on over to talk to her when his smile froze.

Bonnie Grace was buttoning up her top. Even more disturbing was the minxish little smile playing at the edges of her mouth. A tattooed man with long dark hair and a wispy goatee followed her out of the barn an instant later, tugging up the zipper on his black denim pants. The man was one of the few people at the hootenanny he didn't recognize on sight, though he looked like the type prone to hanging out at a biker bar called Stumpy's.

Though he didn't know this particular hooligan, Bob was well-acquainted with his type from his years of working at the car wash next door to Stumpy's. Bloody knife fights in the parking lot were a common occurrence at the disreputable watering hole.

Why someone as sweet and pure as Bonnie Grace would even consider monkeying around with someone so thoroughly unworthy was beyond comprehension. Bob allowed for the possibility that he might be judging the guy in a harsh and unfair way, slotting him in the category of sleazy thug based on nothing other than his appearance. As a person who had spent much of his life being judged solely for his size, wasn't it wrong of him to assume the worst about this man based only on the way he looked?

Maybe.

But then Bob noted the man's smug expression and the way his oily gaze was locked in on Bonnie Grace's shapely bottom.

Then again, maybe not.

Beer sloshed out of the cup he was gripping, dousing his shaking hand.

Herk gasped in surprise. "Whoa, dude."

Bob hadn't even realized he'd been squeezing the cup so hard. He flipped it into the nearest of the several large, plastic-lined trash cans ringing the main party area behind the house, then shook off the excess moisture before wiping his hands on his pants.

Herk gave him a look of concern. "Something wrong, man?"

Bob didn't know what to say.

Something was wrong, but he was reluctant to say what it was because he was starting to feel like a fool. He'd based his assumption that this entrancing woman might be into him on a single brief interaction in a public place. She might only have been so friendly with him because it was the polite thing to do. They'd already known each other in a slightly more than passing way. Walking out without saying a word to a familiar face would have been rude.

And Bonnie Grace wasn't the kind of gal who'd ever be rude without cause, not if she could help it.

But there was that wink.

Yes, the wink, that almost magical moment his mind had

convinced him was imbued with deeper meaning of an amorous nature. But perhaps he'd misconstrued it. It was possible she winked like that at all the men she knew, a reflex, a purely innocent unthinking tic. She could hardly be blamed if a doofus with a crush read more into it than there was.

And yet …

Bob shook his head.

Nope. There was more to it than that. I fucking know it.

What convinced him was the lingering moment of eye contact that came after the wink. She'd been telling him something in that moment, even if she hadn't said anything. There'd been definite interest. But even if he was right about that, a wink wasn't a promise, was it? Nothing in a wink was a guarantee she might not run into some other guy she'd rather hook up with, which was what appeared to have happened.

Bob knew it shouldn't feel so crushing. His built-up expectations weren't anyone's fault but his own. The self-respecting thing to do now would be to shake off the disappointment of it and get on with enjoying his night. Hell, there were lots of fine ladies present. He might yet get lucky.

Herk loudly cleared his throat. "You're not stuck on Bonnie Grace, are you?"

Bob glanced at him, a guarded look on his face. "Let's say a fella was to take a liking to her. Just in theory. What would be wrong with that? Are you implying something?"

Herk took a sip from his cup. "I'm not *implying* anything, good buddy. I'm straight-up *telling* you the lady ain't a lady at all, at least not no proper kind. She's a whore."

Bob's next words emerged with an uncharacteristic tinge of anger. "Are you calling her loose? Ain't that misogynistic as hell, not to mention more than a little hypocritical coming from an unrepentant man-slut such as yourself?"

Herk snorted laughter as he held up a hand in a placating gesture. "Whoa, let's take it down a notch, partner. It ain't misogynistic to say the truth. What I'm trying to tell you is she's literally a whore." He raised his eyebrows, waggling them in a meaningful way. "As in she accepts money in exchange for sexual services. Ya get me? Because I'm pretty sure that's what just happened over yonder."

He indicated the barn with a nod.

Bob gaped at his friend in silence.

Herk's expression softened, turning sympathetic. "Look, man, I know the gal has this wholesome aura about her, like she stepped out of fuckin' *Leave It To Beaver*, but that's a whatchacallit. A fuckin' façade. She hangs out at Stumpy's and Billy Billiards, places like that, has a regular clientele of scuzzy-ass johns. I figured you knew. It's pretty common knowledge."

It hadn't been common knowledge to Bob.

He cast his gaze around, looking again for Bonnie Grace and the skeezy guy who'd followed her out of the barn. It took a moment, but he soon spotted them. The long-haired guy was now at the far periphery of the growing party crowd, hanging close to the edge of the parking area with a cluster of other greasy-looking dudes, likely all regulars at Stumpy's. Taken as a whole, they looked like a giant, amorphous knot of leather, chain wallets, and tattoos.

Bonnie Grace had joined a small group of other ladies who were all sporting nearly identical expressions of mischief, smirking and laughing as they exchanged the latest gossip. The others were all gals he knew by sight. Heather McIntire was an Iraq war widow and mother of four who lived in the Starry Skies trailer park. Bob saw her there often when visiting Dave and Kelsey. Dressed in a tight microskirt and skimpy top with her big boobs hanging out, she was definitely not in mommy mode tonight.

Ashlynn Finnigan was a receptionist at the Ford dealership in town. Sandy Miller was a part-time clerk at the Circle K. Come to think of it, she'd been on duty when he'd bumped into Bonnie Grace last night. He remembered now how she'd smirked at the pack of Trojans he'd added to his purchases at the last minute. Ashlynn and Sandy, like Heather, were dressed in revealingly provocative fashion.

Of the four of them, Bonnie Grace was the only one attired in relatively conservative fashion, basic white cotton shorts with barely noticeable polka dots and a top that was neither too tight nor too small. She would look right at home at a classier backyard gathering in one of the town's wealthier neighborhoods. Whereas here at Walt's hootenanny, she looked out of place in the sea of barely-there outfits that looked ready to burst free of the curvaceous bodies they were struggling to contain. Bonnie Grace's friends all looked like strippers-in-training, as did so many of the other ladies present. Was he really supposed to believe that out of all of them, *she* was the one having sex with strangers for cash?

It didn't seem possible.

Yet he'd never known Herk to lie.

Herk waved a hand in front of Bob's face. "Hello? Anybody home in there?"

Bob blinked and shook his head. "Sorry. I was lost in thought."

Herk groaned. "Man, you've got to let this Bonnie Grace thing go. I hate to be crass about it, but if what I've heard is right, and I think it is, she's had at least a hundred different dicks inside her this year alone. Yeah, I know, she looks like she farts cupcakes and rainbows, but trust me, you don't want any part of that, unless you've got some kind of fucked up kink for contracting STDs."

Bob nodded and started walking away from him.

"Hey, where you goin', man?" Herk called after him, sounding mildly aggrieved. "I'm tellin' you the straight-up truth about that gal. Steer clear."

Bob flipped a hand at him in a gesture of mild dismissal and kept walking, ignoring occasional shouted greetings from some of the other partygoers. His attention was locked on Bonnie Grace, who hadn't noticed him yet as he continued in a straight line toward her group. She appeared deeply immersed in her conversation with the other three ladies, her eyes bright and lively as Heather McIntire yammered on and on about some rich old guy who wanted to marry her and move her and her kids into his big house in Riverside Heights, the rich part of Drayton Falls.

It sounded like a load of shit to Bob, but he wasn't here to rain on her parade. Or anyone else's parade, for that matter.

He just wanted to talk to Bonnie Grace.

Probably he was about to make a huge ass out of himself, a fate his buddy had tried to spare him, but he felt powerless to restrain the urge. The prospect of imminent embarrassment was nothing next to his desperate need to expose Herk's account of her descent into whoredom as incorrect. Not a deliberate falsehood necessarily, as he knew Herk wouldn't do such a thing, but wasn't there at least some small sliver of a chance he was misinformed?

The ladies remained oblivious to his approach even after he'd drawn to within a few feet of them. He was on the verge of clearing his throat to semi-politely disrupt Heather's unending stream-of-consciousness ramble about her supposed rich benefactor when Bonnie Grace's head abruptly turned in his direction.

A big smile spread across her face. "*There* you are. I've been looking all over for you, Bob Abernathy."

Bob grinned. "You have?"

Bonnie Grace excused herself from the conversation with the other women and approached him. She pulled him into a hug and rubbed his back, her face nuzzling the side of his neck as she paid him a few seemingly sincere compliments about how good he looked.

In no way had Bob been prepared for so intimate a clinch. Up to this moment, he'd harbored no serious hope of a revival of the amorous aspirations that had consumed him since last night. He'd expected only more disappointment, a final dashing of faded hopes, but everything felt different now with the softness of her lithe body pressed so firmly against his own. The sweet scent of her perfume made him feel dizzy and disoriented.

She broke the embrace and backed off a step. "You're blushing."

Bob frowned. "Am I?"

But in the next second he realized she was right. His face felt as hot as the core of a nuclear reactor approaching critical meltdown. Sweat formed on his brow and little beads of moisture slid slowly down the sides of his face. The other women watched him with smirking expressions. One of them said, "Oh my god," and the others giggled.

Bonnie Grace ignored them as she took him by the hand. "Walk with me."

He said nothing but allowed her to lead him away from the trio of smirking women. At first he thought she was steering him toward the barn, which brought a troubled expression to his sweat-sheened face. No more than fifteen minutes had passed since he'd seen her buttoning up her top as she'd walked out of the barn ahead of the greasy biker. She seemed genuinely happy about his presence at the party, but was that only because she saw him as prospective customer number two in a long line of men she meant to service before the night was done?

He thought about that thing Herk had said about how she'd had at least a hundred dicks in her since the start of the year and wondered what that count would be up to come sunrise. Maybe she'd worked out an arrangement with Walt in advance of the hootenanny, with him allowing her the use of the decrepit old barn as a sort of pop-up whorehouse in exchange for cutting him in on a slice of her action. Sort of like a backwoods redneck version of *Risky Business*. All her gal pals might be in on it with her. They certainly looked the part. Well, if Bonnie Grace was expecting him to pony up cash for a roll in the literal hay, she could forget it. He had a little more self-respect than that.

His frown deepened.

Well, *maybe* he had more self-respect than that. He'd paid for sex once or twice years ago, back before his big weight loss and extended nuthouse stay, but he'd figured those days were over. He hadn't transformed into some sort of James Bondian playboy, but in general he wasn't nearly as hard up these days.

If Bonnie Grace sensed the increasingly unsettled nature of his thoughts, she showed no sign of it. As she led him past the barn, she squeezed his hand and gave him another of those sweet smiles that made her look like she'd escaped from a '50s sitcom.

Bob glanced backward an instant before they went around the far side of the barn, catching a glimpse of Herk staring after him. His friend's pinched expression was a study in concern. He was clearly worried Bonnie Grace was about to take advantage of his crush on her, disarming him once again with her cultivated aura of All-American wholesomeness. Bob knew the concern was not without legitimate foundation. What he'd seen Bonnie Grace doing earlier was nigh impossible to misinterpret, yet here he was, walking hand-in-hand with her as they continued past the barn and toward a line of trees some thirty feet to the rear of the structure. He was beginning to suspect his hard-earned self-respect might take a serious hit before the night was over.

"Um … Bonnie Grace?"

She glanced at him, flashing another spectacular smile. "Yes, Bob?"

"Where are we going?"

She laughed. "Into the woods, of course. I thought we'd take a nice little walk, get away from the party for a little bit before it gets all crazy later. Have some quiet me and you time. I like you, Bob. I mean, I *really* like you. You know that, right?"

The heat had faded from his cheeks but now a little flush of it crept back in. He managed a trembling, nervous smile as he said. "Well, I like you, too. *Really* like you."

She squeezed his hand. "That's nice. I'm so happy to hear it."

Bob was feeling a little better about things, but his troubled thoughts still had not entirely deserted him. He wanted to believe he'd misunderstood what he'd seen earlier, but the scene kept replaying in his head. Denying the obvious implications was like looking at an apple and swearing it was an orange. Self-delusion on an absurd scale. Then there was the matter of his extreme nervousness in the lady's presence. No girl had caused him to blush like this since he was a middle school virgin. It made him feel like he'd stepped back in time, become that younger, far more awkward version of himself again.

The effect she was exerting on him was damn near hypnotic, as if she had him locked into a tractor beam of erotic allure, exuding a power he had no hope of resisting. Even this basic level of intimacy with Bonnie Grace felt like heaven on earth. Actual sex with her would probably make his head explode from the sheer transcendent ecstasy of it.

They entered the woods and continued walking for a considerable distance, holding hands in conversational silence as Bonnie Grace softly hummed an entrancingly melancholic tune he did not recognize. After a while, the world around him took on a hazy, fuzzy tinge that made him feel the way he did when he was high on strong weed. He felt a bit like he was moving through a dream world, barely conscious of the physical act of walking. At one point, one of his feet snagged on a vine and he nearly stumbled, but somehow Bonnie Grace kept him upright and continued leading him deeper into the forest.

There came a point where Bob realized he could no longer hear the sounds of the rowdy party, the music and all the voices and laughter having become inaudible an indeterminate number of minutes ago. He and Bonnie Grace had been walking together without speaking long enough that it was actually kind of really fucking strange. Every time he felt close to saying something about it, his brain again focused on the unknown tune she'd not stopped humming since they'd entered the woods. As soon as that happened, his thoughts turned fuzzy again.

Another odd thing was how bright everything seemed. By now, full night had fallen. Beneath this canopy of tall, leafy trees, the terrain should be shrouded in deep darkness. Yet it was like they were walking in daylight. If at any point he'd thought to look up, he might have glimpsed the shifting pattern of colored lights emanating from the silent alien spacecraft floating above the trees, but that did not happen.

Not yet.

The fuzziness clouding his thoughts faded somewhat when they entered a small clearing and stopped walking. Bonnie Grace had stopped humming the tune he didn't recognize. Even in the midst of his lingering disorientation, it occurred to him to wonder if the two things might somehow be related. Could the humming have affected his brain somehow, perhaps amplifying the hypnotic power he'd perceived? The idea was like something out of a fairy tale, with Bonnie Grace in the role of a modern Pied Piper. He wanted to dismiss the notion as absurd, but that sense of having temporarily lost control of his own will remained.

Bonnie Grace smiled again as she turned him toward her and pushed him backward in a gentle but insistent way. He stopped when his back pressed up against a large tree. Despite his stirrings of unease, he again felt under her spell, no music necessary this time. A sensation like a mild electric shock came over him as she splayed the fingers of her right hand against his chest and tilted her head backward. The feeling wasn't unpleasant but it was strange, more like a full-body vibration than a snap of static.

The sensation intensified as she maintained the pressure of her fingers against his chest. Another physiological reaction was also occurring, one he wasn't fully cognizant of until the first moan of pleasure escaped his quivering lips. His cock was engorged, and he was writhing against the tree. The hardness was something beyond normal arousal. He felt like he had a brick wedged inside the tight crotch of his jeans. It was strange, because even absent direct physical manipulation of his genitalia, he could feel himself building to climax. He'd be coming in his pants before too much longer if the erotic vibration didn't ease up soon.

As this was happening, he was aware he was in the grip of an unnatural or artificial power beyond his understanding. He was confused and scared, torn between a desperate desire to flee and a perhaps even stronger wish to let Bonnie Grace finish whatever strange thing she was doing, to take him to the point of explosive orgasm and beyond. "Explosive" was an apt word. His cock felt so huge and swollen he feared it really would blow apart like a flesh-bomb once he finally hit that moment of physical release. Trembling on the brink of insanity, he laughed, imagining how it'd feel to experience his life's moment of greatest pleasure and worst, searing pain in the same instant.

A part of his brain was screaming at him to shove Bonnie Grace away and run for his life, but he couldn't move. Her fingers against his chest held him in place as firmly as iron manacles. He was powerless to stop whatever horrendous thing was about to happen. It occurred to him to wonder whether he'd fallen into the clutches of some ancient witch, a powerful hag of folklore hiding behind a beautiful façade, a carefully maintained illusion.

Magic.

For a minute or two, it was the only explanation Bob's fevered brain could comprehend, but soon fresh evidence presented an alternate explanation. One that made more logical sense than ancient sorcery but was infinitely scarier. The first hint of it came when he noted the strange way her eyes were moving beneath her closed eyelids. The movement was nothing like the rapid fluttering of a sleeper deep in a REM state. These movements were more precise, slow clockwise and counterclockwise rotations that looked ... *mechanical.*

A painful lump formed in Bob's throat.

What the fuck is this bitch? She ain't no real lady.

Bob perceived the low whine of some internal mechanism as she tilted her head even more precariously backward, a sound that increased in volume as her mouth stretched slowly open.

"What ... what ... are you ... d-doing?" Bob asked, his words emerging through a strained whimper.

The question was rhetorical. They were just words that popped out, a reflection of his mounting terror. He uttered them with no serious expectation of a reply, but to his great surprise, he got one.

The O-shape of Bonnie Grace's mouth stretched wider as words floated out of the orifice. They were spoken in a voice that was recognizable as her own, but they sounded strangely disembodied, as if uttered through an intercom speaker rather than a human larynx.

The words she spoke were, "Preparing for consummation."

If that was a reference to his own impending orgasm, Bob reckoned consummation was mere seconds away.

His face twisted in a look conveying a grotesque combination of intense sexual ecstasy, extreme terror, and frothing anger. Through most of this bizarre encounter, he'd felt completely out of control of his body, but now he hoped he'd merely been overwhelmed by the force of the power manipulating him. Groaning through gritted teeth, he tried his damnedest to concentrate and break free of that power. He began to raise a trembling fist, hoping he could swing it around with enough force to smash it against Bonnie Grace's throat.

At first he was hopeful as he managed to raise his fist to waist level without much trouble, but after that it got harder. The trembling intensified to an unbearable level with each additional fraction of an inch. The strain in his muscles was extraordinary, as if he were attempting to lift a car off the ground with a one-handed grip. At last, he surrendered to the inevitable, allowing his slackening fist to fall away, the yearning depth of his desperation no match for the power exerted by the thing masquerading as a human woman.

Oblivion was approaching and there was nothing he could do about it. Bob closed his eyes and prayed that the agony, when it came, would not last for long, that the trauma of massive sudden blood loss would send his consciousness hurtling into the great beyond seconds later. Then he opened his eyes again when he heard another mechanical noise, this one louder than the previous sounds.

He gasped in disbelief at the sight of Bonnie Grace's head splitting open in the middle, the top part of it dropping slowly backward as if it were on a hinge. A whirring sound preceded the emergence of a long, thin mechanical arm with a cup-like metal attachment at the end. Bob whimpered and squirmed as the thin metal arm rose higher into the air, swiveled about, and then began to extend toward him.

His mind flashed back to the moment when he'd spotted the greasy biker emerging from the barn, when the man was in the process of zipping up his pants. Had that man gone through what he was experiencing now? He'd seemed fine and not in the least distressed, which didn't seem likely in the aftermath of something like this. Then again, that encounter had occurred in close proximity to a bunch of other potential witnesses. Perhaps the Bonnie-bot had treated the biker to a relatively "normal" transactional sexual experience of the sort Herk had alleged she did on a regular basis, while singling Bob out for ... whatever this was. If so, it cast everything about his interactions with Bonnie in a whole new, far more disturbing light.

He felt preyed upon.

Lured and betrayed.

"Dude," an astonished voice from somewhere to his left intruded. "I think that cup thing is for catching your jizz."

Bob moaned as his head turned in the direction of the voice. "My wang is in great distress, man."

Zeke winced, chuckling as he shook his head. "I can see that, bro. It's like you're pregnant with a cock baby or some shit."

Bob couldn't help it.

He was on the verge of enduring one of the strangest deaths in the history of the human race, but he was laughing. Laughing so hard, in fact, he feared he might prematurely rupture his grotesquely over-inflated penis, but he was no longer sure he cared. Escape might be impossible, but if he could disrupt this fucked up experiment, if that's what it was, there'd be some satisfaction in that. It wasn't much to hold onto, but it was better than nothing.

The whirring sounds emerging from the Bonnie-thing ceased and the metal arm stopped in mid-extension. Bob barely noticed this as he continued laughing it up with the imaginary sleaze metal singer. Then came another whirring sound as the thing's bisected open head rotated to the left. Its eyes opened wide and emitted a pulsing red light.

The light flashed on and off over and over and was accompanied by a series of high-pitched clicking, buzzing, and whistling sounds.

Zeke swigged from his Jack Daniel's bottle, which per usual had materialized well after his arrival on the scene. "Motherfucker sounds like it's trying to connect to AOL circa 1996."

Bob was too young to know the AOL reference from anything other than vaguely recalled movie depictions, but he laughed anyway.

Zeke took another big slug from the bottle and came a few steps closer, face crinkling in concentration as he bent at the waist to study the robot-thing's split-open head. "I think it's confused."

Bob whined as he tried hard to focus on what Zeke was saying. His ongoing struggle to hold back his orgasm made it difficult. "How … how … how do you mean?"

Zeke smirked as he stood up straight again. "Ain't it obvious, man? Think about it."

Bob's sweaty brow furrowed in confusion. "But why …" His features slackened slightly. "Oh."

The robot-thing was confused because he appeared to be interacting with someone it couldn't see. Its computer brain was attempting to analyze the situation in a scientific way. The flashing red light was some kind of infrared thing. It was scanning the area where his attention was focused, looking for a life form hidden behind a cloaking device or whatever. That sounded like something he'd ordinarily dismiss as hokey science fiction bullshit, but having been lured into the woods by a mechanical seductress for the purposes of procuring his man mustard, he was already kind of past the point of skepticism. He suspected the technology used to build the robot was alien in origin. Human technology wasn't nearly this advanced yet. Yet for all its amazing sophistication, it had at least one glaring deficiency.

That being an inability to detect symptoms of mental illness in human beings.

Bob sighed. "It's too bad."

Zeke's smirk melted away. "What is, buddy?"

The rock god's tone carried a tinge of concern, evincing little of his usual callous swagger.

Bob pressed his back harder against the tree, grimacing from the strain of trying not to come. Tears spilled from his eyes. He didn't think he could hold back much longer at all, maybe less than a minute.

Maybe only a few seconds.

He whimpered. "You know ... the whole not real thing. If you were something other than a manifestation of my subconscious, you could whack this thing with your JD bottle."

Zeke smiled. "Bro, don't you know by now? I'm exactly as real as you want me to be. That weird brain of yours is special. You've got talents you don't even know about. If you want my help, close your eyes and think about it real fuckin' hard."

Bob cast a doubtful look his way. "But ... what you're saying ... it's not possible."

Zeke snorted laughter, indicating the robot with a wave of his hand. "Dude, you're being mind-raped by a sex robot from beyond the fuckin' stars. Maybe reconsider your idea of what's possible and what ain't. You're almost out of time. Close your eyes, man. Concentrate as hard as you fuckin' can."

Bob closed his eyes.

He still couldn't quite wrap his head around the idea of Zeke taking on an actual solid, physical form through nothing other than the power of his freaking mind, but at this point, what did he have to lose?

The monstrous form of arousal he was experiencing was painful and frightening, but it was impossible to ignore how mind-shatteringly pleasurable it still was. Despite his fear, he remained a slave to physiology. His body yearned for the ecstasy of release, even if it killed him. Concentrating in the way Zeke instructed didn't feel possible.

He pushed his tongue between his teeth and bit down hard enough to draw blood. Not quite hard enough to chomp the tip of his tongue clean off, but it was more than sufficient to trigger a distracting jolt of searing agony. He screamed as blood filled his mouth and slid toward the back of his throat. The pain allowed him to pull back from the brink of sexual surrender just far enough to do as Zeke said.

He pictured Zeke in his head, his brain automatically reproducing all the preexisting details it'd conjured up over the years in the long process of constructing and refining his imaginary pal. In the past, all those things had occurred on a subconscious level, but now Bob attempted some active revision, adding a bit more muscle to the physique he was picturing, along with making him a bit taller. He tried to see this revision as crisply and clearly as possible. Doing that was the easy part. What he remained uncertain about was how to make the image in his head three-dimensional. To bring it into the world. For a stretch of seconds that felt like an eternity, he was assailed by doubt. What was the process? It couldn't just be a matter of thinking super hard. Could it? He was again on the verge of surrender when he attempted the simplest and most obvious thing he could think of, a strategy he was convinced had no chance of succeeding.

He imagined the enhanced version of Zeke opening a door and walking through it, stepping out of the mind of his creator and into the real world.

An instant later, a loud whoop rang out in the little clearing, a sound followed by Zeke unleashing his heavy metal thunder voice to say, *"YOWZER! ARE YOU READY TO ROCK, YOU TIN-ASS MOTHERFUCKER?"*

Bob opened his eyes in time to see Zeke grab hold of the long metal arm protruding from the robot's split-open head. The robot responded with a piercing sound of high-pitched alarm. Its body twisted about as it tried grappling with the singer. For the first time in a while, the fake Bonnie Grace voice emerged from the split-open head, once again sounding like it was emanating from a speaker. The voice cut in and out, filling with static the way the drive-thru speaker at Big Fiesta Burgers often did. It conveyed a loud warning to release what it called the intake rod immediately or face death by laser incineration.

Zeke evinced no signs of fear as he bent the thin metal arm backward, new muscles flexing as he gave it a hard twist, snapping it in two. The whooping alarm sound braying out of the robot's split-open head increased in volume as the singer tossed the broken piece of the arm aside and knocked the robot to the ground. Before it could get back to its feet, he grabbed the robot by its ankles, dragged it into the center of the clearing, and began spinning it around in a circle, picking up speed with each revolution.

The robot's split-open head began emitting a loud sound of caterwauling distress, conveying an almost human-like sense of terror. Its arms lengthened by breaking into segments, hands detaching from wrists, forearms from elbows, exposing the gleaming machinery and circuits beneath the synthetic flesh. The separated pieces extended along sliding metallic rods and tubing. By the time the extension process was complete, the robot's arms were more than twice the length of normal human arms.

And infinitely more flexible.

The arm segments twisted and rotated in multiple directions in an attempt to compensate for the centrifugal force being generated by Zeke's high-speed spinning. The singer was turning so fast his physical form was blurring. Just as the robot's grasping hands were about to close around his throat, he released his grip on its ankles and sent it flying across the clearing. The robot flailed wildly with its crazy, multi-angled arms, but it was unable to alter or impede the trajectory of its airborne path.

Bob winced at the loud crunch that came a fraction of a second later as the top of the robot's head slammed into the wide base of the tallest tree ringing the clearing. Force of impact flattened the head and pulverized a significant portion of the torso. What remained of the machine dropped to the ground and didn't move. It gave out a few last clicks and beeps before going silent.

Zeke raised his arms to the sky as he slowly stopped spinning. He looked like a flesh-and-blood version of a child's spinning top as the energy that set it in motion began to expend itself. He whooped again and pounded his fists against his bare chest.

The grin that pasted itself across Bob's face as he watched this infectiously exuberant display faltered when he perceived the droning, warbling sound generated by some other strange machine, one he had not yet glimpsed. Even with the demise of the Bonnie-bot, the artificial light filling the clearing had not diminished. If anything, it was brighter than ever.

And getting brighter.

Seconds later, he realized the source of both the light and the theremin-like sound emanated from some huge object directly overhead. He gasped as he looked upward and saw the spinning, shimmering underside of the alien spacecraft. His mouth dropped open in mesmerized amazement as he observed the shifting rainbow pattern of light playing across the shimmery metal.

A dark hole irised open in the center of the spinning disc, and a moment later a beam of neon-green light was projected downward into the center of the clearing. Nothing further happened at first, aside from that warbling sound getting louder, but then Zeke began to lift slowly into the air, along with the damaged remains of the sexbot.

Something lurched in Bob's chest.

He stepped forward, raising a hand toward the formerly imaginary friend who'd saved his life tonight. "No!"

Zeke glanced down at him, the look on his face serene, unworried. "Chill, my dude, all will be well. Remember what you did and how you did it. You can always bring me back, if you want." He made a '70s-style "hang loose" hand gesture as he continued to rise upward. "In the meantime, you should probably start running right about now."

This was probably good advice, but for a bit longer, Bob felt incapable of anything other than gawking up at the alien craft, a thing he found amazing and terrifying in equal measures. That it was extraterrestrial in nature was beyond doubt. He was looking at undeniable proof that life did exist on other worlds, something a lot of people a lot smarter than him had spent their lives searching for without success. That it was not, in this case at least, benevolent life was almost beside the point. Mankind was not alone in the universe, and he was among the few who could testify to the fact with absolute conviction.

The fear that had consumed him earlier did not begin to return until he sensed a new wave of energy invade the clearing, bathing his body in a warmth that made him feel lightheaded.

Then Zeke was shouting at him again, screaming, utilizing that thunder voice for one final earthshaking exhortation.

"RUN, MOTHERFUCKER, RUN!"

Bob slapped himself and staggered backward.

The resultant pain focused him, clarified things. When he looked up and saw the craft again, the feeling of wonder that had held him in place vanished, leaving only bone-deep terror in its place.

He turned and ran into the woods, moving with greater ease and speed than he'd thought possible, especially with the rapid fading of the unnatural light that had pervaded the forest. He was guided by blind instinct and a burning need to get far, far away from the alien craft. Along the way, he belatedly realized he was aided in this effort by a total reversal of the physical symptoms inflicted on him by the now destroyed sex robot. He was no longer carrying a cock baby in the crotch of his jeans. For a brief, knee-weakening moment, he panicked, fearing it'd exploded just as he'd feared, somehow without pain. He came to a lurching stop and opened his pants to check. Upon determining that his equipment was intact and had merely shriveled back to a normal size, he took off running again.

Somewhere around ten minutes from the start of his flight back through the woods, he emerged from the forest and groaned in relief when he saw the back of the decrepit barn and heard the party noises from the other side. The relief he felt then was massive, like waking up from a bad dream.

He stood there and listened for a while, breathing hard from his exertions as he wondered what his next move should be.

Zeke was gone, but what could he do about that? He couldn't go to the cops and file a report because as far as the authorities were concerned, Zeke wasn't a real person. He had no social security number. There was no hospital record of his birth because he hadn't been born in the normal sense. The rock god was purely a product of his own mind, a figment, only it was one he'd somehow turned real because it turned out he had some kind of fucked up superpower he'd never known about until tonight.

He couldn't tell the cops any of that, nor could he warn them of a possible space invasion. The law would deem him crazy, maybe even get a court order to slap him back in the loony bin for another extended stay.

An invasion would happen or it wouldn't. In that regard, all he could do was hope for the best. Heck, maybe the aliens weren't as scary as they seemed. Instead of invaders, perhaps they were only simple explorers or scientists, here to collect data and observe life on earth.

That wasn't quite the vibe he got, but ... maybe.

Besides, there were Zeke's parting words to consider.

He'd used his mind to bring Zeke into the flesh-and-blood world once already. It stood to reason he could do it again. The prospect, however, came with a set of mildly disturbing existential implications. If he focused his mind and made Zeke walk through that door again, would it be the same Zeke that had gone up into the alien craft or a copy?

Did it even matter?

Bob sighed.

He had no answers.

It came to him that what he needed more than anything else was something to take his mind off it all. Something to make him forget, at least for a while. A large intake of beer was always an excellent means of accomplishing that particular goal.

Heaving a breath, Bob resumed walking back toward the party.

He smiled as he stepped around the corner of the barn. The hootenanny was still in full swing. The beer was flowing and the music was rocking.

More of the usual shouts of greeting rang out as Bob rejoined the fray.

His buddy Herk spotted him and came over with a fresh cup of cold beer, which Bob accepted with a grateful sigh. He'd worked up a mean, mean thirst from his panicked run through the woods.

Herk chuckled as he watched Bob quaff half the beer down in one long pull. "That's the spirit, man. Belushi that shit. Hey, you missed all the excitement. You'll never believe this, but we're all pretty sure we saw a got-dang UFO go zipping across the sky."

Overhearing this, a skeptic in the vicinity piped in. "Probably just a drone or experimental top-secret military shit."

Bob smiled in a cryptic way as he finished off his beer, which was far from the last he'd have over the course of that wild and wooly night.

"I wouldn't be so sure about that."

Herk tilted his head, giving him a quizzical look. "What do you mean?"

Bob's smile got bigger and bigger. "Gather round, boys, because have I got a story for you, and I swear every word of it is true."

HE WALKS
AT NIGHT

THE MAN KNOWN IN DRAYTON Falls as either He Who Walks at Night, the Eastside Phantom, or simply the Phantom since the middle of the 1990s was out for a late-night stroll for the first time in a long while. His first in the spooky prowler persona he'd created almost by accident long ago, that is. There'd been occasional other post-midnight rambles in the interim, but always without the distinctive handsewn mask and black garb of the Phantom.

The reason for the persona's long absence was simple. He was older and slower than he'd been a few years ago, to the point where it was no longer easy to evade attention or elude those who pursued him. The slippery athleticism of his youth was now just a lamentably faded memory. Even at the peak of his nocturnal wanderings, when he'd gone out walking as the Phantom on a regular basis for years, the percentage of people who caught him in the act of spying on them was quite low. Even on those rare occasions when it *did* happen, his so-called "victims" or their spouses almost never gave chase. More often there was only a shriek of surprise followed by a shouted threat to call the police.

Those he peeped on tended to stay inside if they happened to spot him looking through their windows, because evidently, few people felt it wise to chase after a masked man in the middle of the night.

OUT COME THE FREAKS

That said, while incidents of pursuit were rare, they had happened from time to time, mostly in those younger, more daring years. It was almost always a result of pushing his luck, staring too long through a window even after being spotted. An angry husband or boyfriend would come bursting out of whatever house the Phantom had crept up on, sometimes brandishing a baseball bat or golf club. Most often they stopped at the edge of their own yard after chasing him away, but some of his most cherished memories from those days were the closer calls.

Some among that handful of especially determined pursuers had chased him across numerous yards and streets, forcing him to vault over fences and crash through thick hedges. One time the black cape he'd worn as part of his costume those first few years had snagged on the top of a tall privacy fence after he'd gone over it. The man chasing him was at the top of the fence, ready to drop. In order to escape, he'd been forced to tear free of it, throwing it over the head of his bewildered pursuer when the man dropped to the ground. The maneuver gave him just enough time to sprint across the yard and vault over the fence on the other side. In the process, he eluded a large, snarling dog, but the man chasing him was not so lucky. The shriek of pain that rang out as he was running away brought a huge grin to the Phantom's face. Afterward, he felt exhilarated, his heart pounding as he rode an adrenaline high like nothing else he'd experienced before or since then.

A photo of the Phantom's lost cape appeared in the afternoon paper the following day, accompanying what was one of the first written accounts of his after-hours adventures. He was a known quantity even before then, the subject of several police reports filed by aggrieved citizens and already a source of fervent rumor and gossip, but it was that article—and subsequent ones that appeared intermittently in the coming years—that propelled him to a new level of local notoriety. After that, he became a boogeyman of sorts, one school kids told stories about to scare each other.

Because he never broke into any of the houses he peeped into and never intentionally caused physical harm—the dog attack incident being the only time anyone got hurt—he was regarded as more of a benign annoyance than an actual threat. The Phantom was okay with this perception because he truly had no interest in hurting anyone.

Spooking them, though?

Well, that was another story altogether.

He loved that shit. *Lived* for it.

In the beginning, his late-night wanderings had another purpose. There'd been no plan to become the Phantom. As a young man in his later twenties, he'd been almost suicidally unhappy. His life was inhibited by a profound social awkwardness. He was too shy to talk to women and had only ever been on one formal date in his life, that single occasion being an unmitigated disaster. Even now, all these many years later, he was still a virgin. These days it didn't bother him. He was what he was and he was resigned to it, but back then he still harbored aspirations of being normal and having relationships. He started going on his late-night walks as a way of clearing his head. The stillness of those suburban nights soothed him, lifted some of the crushing weight of existence.

Then one night, several weeks into his night walking, he took a can of black spray paint with him. This was sheer impulse. The paint can was left over from an art project he'd attempted the previous year, another in a long series of failed efforts at redirecting the darkness inside him into something positive.

By then he was already wearing all black when he went out and had the vaguest stirrings of cultivating an identity centered around his excursions, though he'd not yet made his mask. This would be the first time he left evidence of what he was up to in his wake. He still well remembered the anxiety he'd felt upon setting out that night, how difficult it'd been to psyche himself up to committing those initial acts of public defacement and vandalism. The way he got past that mental hurdle was by deciding he'd kill himself if he didn't do it. In the end, he left variations of the same basic message in three places that night.

On the side of a tall white fence, he used his spray can to write *The Phantom Walks.*

He also left messages at sidewalk locations on different streets, one of which read, "He who walks at night," while the other merely said, "He walks."

The shorter version wasn't intentional. Instead, it was cut short by his first ever close call with apprehension. He'd been in the midst of leaving his message on a section of sidewalk right outside the biggest house on the street. Right as he was completing the tail end of the lowercase "s," a flood of high-wattage exterior lighting came on and the front door opened. A burly-looking tall man clad only in boxer shorts stepped out and screamed at him.

OUT COME THE FREAKS

"Get the fuck out of here before I kick your scrawny little ass, you stupid fucking kid!"

He ran away as fast as his feet would take him.

In the aftermath of that incident, he commenced a more serious contemplation of developing his persona and costume, having decided he'd never again go out as the Phantom without some unique means of covering his face. He came up with a simplistic but creepy design and made a mask, stitching it together from pieces of fabric he had on hand. The mask was black with sewn-in silver areas around the eyes. The silver pieces were large and teardrop-shaped, and from a distance they looked quite eerie in dim lighting. One woman who spotted him while in the process of undressing for bed told the newspaper she initially thought she was being peeped on by a creature from another planet. The same woman was also quoted as saying the incident had scared her "nearly to death." Almost literally. Her panic attack was so severe an ambulance was summoned to take her to the hospital.

All this time later, that was still among his most prized newspaper clippings, one that became worn nearly to the point of disintegration from being unfolded and reread so often. These days it was safely preserved in a scrapbook he could look at as often as he liked with no fear of inflicting further damage to the wrinkled scrap of newsprint.

He continued to refine his costume, adding in a black fedora—the first of several he went through over the decades—the long-lost cape, black leather gloves, and a black cane. Everything was always black, save for the silver teardrops. It made melting away into the shadows so much easier. The cane felt like a particularly inspired touch, an appropriate complement to the "gentleman prowler" self-image that had taken shape in his head, but it also had some heft to it. In a pinch, it would serve well as a means of fending off—in a non-lethal way—any pursuer who got too close. He never carried a real weapon like a knife or a gun. The way he saw it, that would be asking for trouble of a sort far beyond the relatively safer kind he courted on a regular basis.

The only thing that annoyed him about his public image was that his preferred moniker was never widely embraced. He liked being "The Phantom" because of the built-in association with popular culture figures like The Phantom of the Opera and the old comic strip character also called the Phantom. His costume was tailored around that image. Unfortunately, when people talked about him, he was almost always referred to as "He Who Walks at Night.".

It was his fault, of course, the public's nickname of choice deriving from the slogans he'd spraypainted across numerous neighborhoods in those first years. What happened was it became a self-replicating thing. Garden variety juvenile delinquents followed his example, defacing sidewalks and overpasses all over the county with his words. For a long while, it became nearly as ubiquitous as other pieces of meme-like graffiti had in other places during other eras. It was like the Drayton Falls version of "Kilroy was here." Often it was accompanied by a simple, cartoon-like depiction of his mask.

For a brief time, he became so irritated by this that he attempted a rebrand as The Night Walker, but early on he saw how clearly doomed the effort was and abandoned it. Over time he made peace with it. In his mind, he was the Phantom, but to everyone else the other name was the only one that mattered.

So be it.

But all that was settled many years ago.

He was more than a quarter century down the line from his most active period of night rambling. There was a new generation of Drayton Falls kids who likely didn't know a lot about him because of the increasingly rare nature of his outings. Maybe they heard stories from their older relations now and then, but the days when he'd been a hot topic of conversation at dinner tables and holiday gatherings were long gone. He supposed the curiosity of the young ones might be stirred enough to question their parents on the subject after spotting some of that faded old graffiti, but a lot of it had disappeared, having either been scrubbed away or painted over.

It made him a little sad to think about sometimes. The passage of time was a merciless thief, taking everything from everyone in the end. Being the Phantom had always required health and vigor. He'd done his best to maintain those qualities at a high level for a long time, but eventually he was forced to reconcile with the physical realities of advancing age.

He'd slowed down.

Only a little at first, then more and more every year, the recent rapid acceleration of his decline alarming him enough to slide into a state of grudging semi-retirement. Over the last year, the only walks he'd taken were in his own neighborhood and always during the day in his regular citizen attire. None of his neighbors questioned the black cane he walked with because they knew he needed it thanks to the debilitating arthritis that made his knees swell and throb so painfully.

In recent days, he'd done a lot of thinking about things. Perhaps the time had come to retire as the Phantom for real, to consign that era of his life permanently to the dustbin of the past. The conclusion he eventually arrived at was that this was the only dignified thing to do. He also gave serious thought to turning his remaining energies to writing a memoir detailing his secret nocturnal life, then arranging to have it posthumously published once he was finished.

This sounded like a fine idea to him.

The book might only ever be read by a small group of people in the local community, but that was okay. All that mattered was that his story would be told and preserved in posterity. It would be a clear-eyed account that set all the facts straight once and for all, debunking all the false rumors and theories while telling nothing but the honest truth about his life. The more he thought about the project, the more enthused he became about it.

The book would be called *I Am the Phantom*.

He loved the declarative and self-affirming nature of the title, believing it would do for him in death what he'd not been able to accomplish in life, finally elevating his preferred name in the consciousness of the public.

He couldn't wait to get started on it.

To mark the occasion of having arrived at this momentous point in his life, he decided he would don the mask one more time and set out on one final walk as the Phantom. Before he could do that, however, he would need to select the right neighborhood for his last outing.

Taking his Phantom gear with him, he got in his car—the same black Lincoln Continental he'd been driving since the '90s—and went out driving. He cruised through a few different neighborhoods on the east side of Drayton Falls, which was one of the nicer parts of town. The area was no Riverside Heights, that hoity toity enclave of the genuinely affluent, but it was clean and pretty, the neighborhood streets an endlessly unfurling series of well-tended lawns like something out of a perfect Disney vision of idealized suburbia. There was nary a trace of the deep decay that characterized, for example, the south side, where all the hicks and criminals lived.

After becoming the Phantom, he'd never restricted his

wanderings to a single location. If he'd done that, his career of prowling would likely have come to a much earlier end. Though a mental
health professional might well diagnose him as having certain psychological disorders, one thing he decidedly was *not* was stupid. Evad-
ing apprehension during his more daring early years hadn't entirely
been a matter of utilizing athleticism. Just as important was the way
he'd expanded his area of operations. East side neighborhoods were
his primary preference, but he'd done walks throughout most of
Drayton Falls, with the perpetual exception of neighborhoods on the
south side. Doing a Phantom Walk at, for example, the seedy Starry
Skies trailer park struck him as a supremely unwise idea.

Courting a little bit of excitement and—mostly—low-level danger
was one thing. He'd long ago assessed the relative risks involved in
doing his thing in respectable neighborhoods and deemed them ac-
ceptable. At the same time, he saw no good reason to put himself in
a position where there was a real possibility of being mugged or
worse. He might have considered it early on, when he was so plagued
by thoughts of worthlessness and suicidal ideation, but not since then.

Which was why it was so strange to find himself heading out toward the southernmost part of Drayton Falls after cruising through
so many pristine east side neighborhood streets. He supposed he was
being propelled by a last little flicker of that old inner darkness, that
original spark of wild inspiration. It made him nervous but also
brought back some of the live-wire excitement he used to feel when
setting off on his adventures.

Besides, despite the way it was perceived throughout the rest of
the county, the south side wasn't entirely comprised of rundown
trailer parks, seedy pay-by-the-week motels, and dumpy apartment
buildings. He hadn't been out that way in a long time, but he knew
there were at least a couple of semi-okay proper neighborhoods. The
houses there were much older and not as nice as in other parts of
town, but the people who lived in them tended to be far less shady
than other denizens of the south side.

Or at least that was the case years and years ago.

Whether that was still true was something he meant to see for
himself.

At right around half past one in the morning, he pulled his Lincoln
Continental into a neighborhood a faded sign identified as Kingston
Hills. It was a funny name for a place that wasn't perceptibly hilly, but
he supposed it'd sounded good to the developers who'd chosen it

way back in the early 1950s. He cruised slowly through the streets, seeing nothing that set off any alarms. Though he saw an odd light or two on here and there, the houses were mostly dark, their residents asleep and recharging for another day of whatever type of drudge work they did during daylight hours. No one was out wandering the streets.

Well, that last part was about to change.

After his brief tour of the neighborhood, he returned to the entrance and parked the Lincoln behind the faded sign. The sign wasn't quite large enough to fully hide the vehicle from view, but he doubted anyone would notice it there in the dead of night.

He pulled on his mask, perched the fedora atop his head, grabbed his cane, took one last big, calming breath, and got out of the car. After a final moment of nervous hesitation, he stepped out from behind the big sign and started walking the quiet streets of Kingston Hills. There was an initial jitteriness that quickened his breath and made his heart beat maybe a little too hard, but after he'd traversed a couple of blocks without incident, that feeling began to fade.

At an intersection, he took a left turn and continued in the same largely nonchalant manner for another block. The houses he passed were still mostly dark. He was struck by what an ordinary neighborhood it was in so many ways, yet there were also clear indications it was a different kind of place from his usual stomping grounds. Some of the yards were overgrown while others were littered with children's toys. Even the lawns that were recently mown had a general unkemptness at the edges. It was evident no one here gave a damn about preserving a perfect Disney lawn. Also, there were no sidewalks. He had to walk on the streets, which was fine.

He'd walked for more than fifteen minutes before deciding he felt at ease enough to entertain the idea of peeping on someone. On impulse, he stopped outside the next house he came to with a light on in one of the windows. Two cars were parked outside the house—an old Pontiac Firebird in the gravel driveway and, at the edge of the yard, a sleek black sports car of a far more recent vintage. The emblem on the front identified it as some model of Mercedes. The presence of this symbol of wealth in a place like Kingston Hills intrigued him but also triggered a stirring of trepidation. It was strange enough to make him seriously consider moving on to the next house with a lighted window.

In the end, his curiosity overcame his concerns.

He started across the spongy ground of the patchy lawn. Judging from the ridged lines zigzagging across it, the resident here had a bad mole problem. He kept going, angling toward the far-right end of the house. It was a side window, presumably one for a bedroom. If a woman lived here and was awake at this late hour, there was a better than even chance he'd get to see her in a state of at least semi-undress. His shriveled old cock twitched a little at the image this put in his head. There'd always been a little bit of a sexual aspect to his habit of creeping and peeping, but throughout his career as the Phantom, he'd never once given any serious thought to breaking in and assaulting any of the women he spied on. Just the idea of that sickened him. He accepted that he was a strange person, the type many would label a "perv" or a creep, but he wasn't a monster. The Phantom was a playful boogeyman, not a rapist.

All of which was one-hundred percent true, but what he *would* often do was keep the images of the scantily-clad and occasionally nude women he peeped on in his head long enough to return home and masturbate to them.

What harm was there in that?

The Phantom grinned behind his mask.

None whatsoever.

After arriving at the lighted window, he put his masked face close to the glass and was able to see into the room. A closed blind covered most of the window, but there was a vertical sliver of space to peep through between the edge of the window and the edge of the blind.

He saw right away that the room was indeed a bedroom, one with a four-poster bed, plush blue carpeting, and walls painted a faint shade of pink. A boxy black television from the days before hi-def sat atop a tall chest of drawers. Next to the chest of drawers was a small table and an oval-shaped vanity mirror. It was a perfectly ordinary room.

What was not so ordinary was the upsetting thing taking place on the floor in front of the four-poster bed. It was like a lurid scene out of a sleazy B-grade horror movie. The unexpected sight so shocked him that his brain was briefly unable to accept or process it as real.

A slender woman in a black ski mask sat astride another woman clad in lacy pink lingerie. The woman in the mask was wearing the outfit of a cheerleader. Grasped tightly in her gloved right hand was a shiny meat cleaver already wet with blood. As the Phantom's eyes widened in horror, the masked woman raised the cleaver high above her head and brought it down with tremendous force. The blade chopped through the arm of the woman pinned to the floor, nearly severing it below the shoulder in just one blow. Blood pumped out of the wound in alarming spurts as the masked assailant raised the blade again and brought it down a second time. The second chop completed the severing of the woman's arm. Her attacker swept the limb aside as blood continued to pump out and stain the carpet. The woman on the floor looked like she was screaming or trying to scream, but something was stuffed in her mouth, an object large enough to puff out her cheeks.

The Phantom's terror of what he was witnessing was so extreme he didn't realize he was on the verge of collapse until he slumped against the brick wall, bumping his forehead against the window. The masked woman's head snapped toward him. Beautiful blue orbs bulged behind the eyeholes. Her hand was high up in the air again, the bloody cleaver poised to inflict another horrendous wound. Their eyes met through the sliver of open space for a fraction of a second.

Then the woman in the cheerleader costume got to her feet and started moving fast toward the bedroom's open door. On the floor, the dying woman's tear-streaked, puffy face rolled toward the window. The Phantom perceived a faint glimmer of desperate hope. He felt sorry for her, but he was not here to play rescuer.

He took a few quick backward steps, then turned around and started moving as fast as he could toward the street, which he'd nearly reached when he heard the front door of the house bang open. Somewhere in the distance, a street or two over, a dog barked in reaction to the sound. During his active prowling days, he'd always gone about his business as stealthily as possible, moving as quietly and nimbly as a cat so as not to provoke the ire of neighborhood canines. Now he welcomed the sound and hoped other dogs would take up the lead of the first, working themselves into a frenzy of barking. The ruckus might wake up other residents and prompt them to look outside, perhaps even place a call to 911. After decades of trying to avoid them, he hoped the police would come. The risk of apprehension and possible exposure was meaningless next to the prospect of painful, violent death at the hands of a madwoman.

As soon as his feet hit asphalt, he did his best to pick up the pace, the tip of his cane thumping repeatedly against the ground as he poured every ounce of will he had into the effort. His face twisted with pain as his swollen knees protested the unusual level of exertion.

Breathing became difficult and his chest felt tighter than a nun's pussy, as one of his high school bullies used to say. Not that he could attest to the veracity of such a thing from personal experience, of course. Every step was an agonized labor.

The woman in the mask caught up to him with little discernible effort, falling into step behind him shortly after bursting out of the house. He sensed her following along at what was for her an unhurried, nonchalant pace. The Phantom's eyes filled with tears as he realized he had zero chance of outrunning or eluding her. He nonetheless kept plodding forward, whimpering from the worsening strain. Despite knowing how bleak his plight was, he couldn't stop, his awakened survival instinct stronger than he ever would have guessed. It was such a shame his body wasn't nearly so strong.

The Phantom and his pursuer continued down the street in near silence for at least another full minute. He had the sense the deranged woman was enjoying the sluggish chase. She was a black widow spider taking her time with a pitiful bug that'd had the misfortune to wander into her web.

Then she chuckled and said, "I always wondered if I'd run into you one of these nights, out here in these dirty fucking streets."

The Phantom whimpered and glanced over his shoulder, eyes widening upon realizing she was closer even than he'd guessed. "Y-you ... know me?"

He saw her grin widen behind the mouth-hole of the mask.

She nodded. "You are He Who Walks. The Phantom. The Night Walker."

The Phantom sniffled.

His dark heart warmed a little at hearing her say these things. She knew his history, even remembered his forgotten rebrand attempt. Was it possible she was a fan, a devotee of Phantom Lore? His mind was buzzing as he slowed his pace slightly. He was still wary of this woman, an obvious psychopath, but if she had respect for him on some level, might she spare him her dark wrath?

She laughed like she'd read his thoughts and shook her head. "Stop walking, Mr. Phantom. You're embarrassing yourself."

The Phantom took a final lurching step forward, then did as she said.

After coming to a halt, he heaved a weary, exhausted breath and turned toward her, grunting from the pain.

The masked opponents stood facing each other in heavy,

portentous, almost reverential silence for a last few moments.

Then the woman in the cheerleader outfit raised the cleaver above her head as she came another step closer. "Tonight I give you a new name, Mr. Phantom. You need one because you are clearly no longer a phantom at all. Look at you." She shook her head, sighing heavily in obvious disgust. "Hobbled by an old man's ailment. Too timid to ever do anything more serious than creep around and say boo. This is a new era that calls for boldness, and that's where I come in."

She brought the cleaver down with all her might, swinging the blade at an angle that caused it to chop halfway through his throat. He gargled and hissed, dropping his cane as his empty hands clawed uselessly at the air. The masked woman held the blade in his violated flesh for a protracted moment before tearing it out, allowing blood to spray from the devastating wound.

The dying man dropped to his knees.

The masked woman laughed and raised the cleaver again.

"Tonight I call you ... He Who Dies."

She slammed the cleaver down, leaving it embedded in his flesh as the Phantom toppled over and continued bleeding out on the dirty asphalt.

Angela Conroy gave some thought to removing the man's head and taking it with her as a gruesome souvenir, but the barking of the dogs was getting louder and more lights were coming on up and down the street. She felt mildly irritated at having her fun interrupted, but she'd make up for it when she got home. It'd been a while since she'd taken the poor thing that lived in the cage in her basement out for a prolonged play session anyway.

The thought made her smile as she slid in behind the wheel of her Mercedes, started the engine, and drove out of the disgusting poor people's neighborhood.

She also consoled herself with the knowledge of the absolutely momentous thing she'd done tonight.

It wasn't every day you got to kill a town's boogeyman, to vanquish a true local legend, but she'd done just that.

But that was the natural way of things, wasn't it?

As one scary old legend fades into obscurity, a new one must rise in its place.

And the legend of Angela Conroy, aka the Drayton Falls Slasher, was just beginning.

OUT COME THE FREAKS

Excerpt

aka The Freakshow II, actual title TBD

THERE'S A HINT OF SOMETHING wild in the air tonight.

Can you feel it?

It's a bit like that strange tingling feeling you sometimes get ahead of a big storm. You know what I mean, the one that feels like a mild electrical current rolling over your skin. It raises gooseflesh and makes old bones ache. At the same time, a profound stillness settles over the land, heavy with portent. It's ominous, as if the world is holding its breath, anticipating the unleashing of powerful forces. Forces that gather only to wreak havoc and destruction. A monster hurricane of the sort Mother Nature has seen fit to inflict on some regions with increasing frequency in recent years, for instance.

Yeah, this wildness is a bit like that.

But it's also something more.

Because in this case that anticipatory feeling is imbued with a distinct sense of *wrongness*. Something bad is coming, but it's not a storm. It's something worse, an encroaching malevolence that pulsates with malignant corruption. Most folks when they feel it lack the ability to articulate exactly what that thing is, but they grasp that it is something outside the realm of ordinary experience and understanding. It's an *alien* feeling, like something from another world or dimension, a perception some among us are too willing to dismiss as baseless paranoia or plain silliness. That's just human nature. It's fear at its most primal manifesting as urgent denial.

My advice?

Don't ever ignore that feeling.

Tonight I'll tell you the story of the time the Flaherty Brothers Traveling Carnivale and Freakshow came to Drayton Falls and brought with it a poisonous connection to a world beyond this one, a dying place its malformed and rapaciously evil inhabitants call the Nothing. These are the Freaks, and they despise those of us fortunate enough to have been born in this world rather than the Nothing.

The carnival departed this region some while ago, moving on as it always does after infecting small communities with some of its rot, but rumor has it a few stray Freaks remained behind, disappearing into these woods where they remain to this day.

Again … as rumor has it.

And I'll tell you something.

I believe the rumors.

In fact, I believe at least one of the wayward creatures might be nearby this very night, lurking behind the trees surrounding our little campsite. Maybe more than just one. They're the source of that spark of strange wildness and foreboding in the air I mentioned earlier. Now, don't let it bother you overly much. I know the secret to keeping them at bay. You'll be safe as long as you stay here with me tonight.

In the meantime, let's all scoot a little closer to the fire. Just hunker down and get warm and comfortable, maybe have another taste or two of your favorite libation.

This is where our story starts.

~

The traveling carnival just showed up one day. Not so much as a single flyer was pasted up anywhere in town in the days and weeks ahead of its arrival in Drayton Falls. The lack of advance advertising struck some as odd, though not to a degree that merited any serious level of concern. Most people, if they gave the matter any thought at all, chalked it up to budget issues, the carnival clearly being a shoestring operation. The people in charge likely preferred to rely on good old-fashioned word-of-mouth. In all likelihood, this approach was just as effective as papering a town with cheap flyers and for sure a whole lot less expensive.

You see, people are easily charmed by the quaintness of an

independent traveling carnival, which is no longer a common enterprise. Among many, it sparks a fuzzy nostalgia or yearning for an earlier, more innocent era, even if those experiencing that feeling are too young to have been a part of that bygone time.

"A sucker is born every minute," the old saying goes, and that's just the plain truth.

The word gets out and the rubes show up.

Every damn time.

The trucks and long-haul trailers the Flaherty Brothers company used for transporting equipment were all multiple decades old at the least, as were the numerous concession and bunkhouse trailers. Several of the vehicles sported fading painted logos. All were covered in layers of grime and road dust from many years of traveling the rural byways of the southern and midwestern parts of the country, as well as some strange routes you won't find printed on any map.

It's fair to say that many queuing up on opening night in Drayton Falls felt like they'd stepped out of the modern age and into the past, as if they'd passed through an invisible magic portal upon entering the parking lot of the abandoned shopping center where the carnival had set up shop. More than a few patrons experienced something similar but subtly different, a strange sense they'd stepped not just back in time, but into another world entirely. The feeling made its presence known in the form of a mildly unpleasant prickling at the back of the neck, a sensation akin to the mild shock of static electricity. It was felt most sharply by that small percentage of especially sensitive individuals in attendance.

One of whom was Penny Reed.

Having recently turned fifteen, Penny was not overly thrilled about being dragged along to the dinky carnival by her older sister, Haley. It was so unfair. Haley was older, yes, but if anything, she was far less emotionally mature than her decade-younger sibling. She was an impulsive risk-taker who'd had multiple minor run-ins with the law, the worst of which netted her a hefty fine and some compulsory community service.

Their parents didn't care about any of that, though. A few days earlier they'd left to go on a two-week cruise to the Bahamas and had left Haley in charge, departing with a stern admonishment for Penny to obey her sister like a stand-in parent.

Penny didn't get it. *She* wasn't the one still living at home several years after graduating high school. As a student, she was the absolute opposite of her delinquent sister. Long ago labeled as "gifted" by teachers and counselors, her grades were perfect. She'd never once been in any kind of trouble. A bright future at some quality university outside of Drayton Falls loomed on the not-too-distant horizon. Yet none of that impressed her parents, who treated their eldest—and admittedly prettier—daughter like a golden Hollywood starlet. The fact she'd never accomplished anything of any genuine note in no way diminished their glowing perception of Haley.

They deferred to her in all ways on everything.

It wasn't just unfair, it was fucked up.

As their group neared the booth where tickets were being sold, Haley dug into her purse and pulled out a half-empty pint bottle of Southern Comfort. After screwing off the cap and taking a quick swig, she pushed the bottle into Penny's hands and said, "Drink up, little sis."

Penny's face twisted in disdain as she eyed the bottle. This was far from the first time Haley had tried to peer pressure her into drinking. On most previous occasions, she'd managed to resist, but a few times she'd caved in the face of persistent and aggressive badgering. She'd never taken more than a few grudging sips at a time, a more than sufficient sampling to conclude that whiskey—and possibly alcohol in general—was not for her. Yet Haley kept trying, pushing it off on her every chance she got, laughing off her sister's complaints about the taste. She was engaged in a relentless effort to wear her down and was always telling her she needed to be less of a loser nerd. It was a little sad, maybe even kind of pathetic, because Penny was pretty sure she wasn't the loser in this equation.

Her parents would see that one day, surely, even if it was years down the road.

She shook her head and tried giving the bottle back. "I don't want any."

Haley rolled her eyes. "Oh, come on, stop being so fucking lame. You need to learn to loosen up and party like a normal person."

She pushed the bottle back into Penny's hands, making her close her fingers around the curved sides of the slim bottle.

Penny's lips pooched out, quivering as a crease formed in her brow. "I really don't want to."

Haley heaved an exaggerated sigh and shook her head. "I can't believe how ungrateful you are. I'm just trying to teach you to be cool. What the fuck is wrong with you? Don't you *want* to be popular?"

Penny's eyes glimmered with moisture. The trembling of her bottom lip became more pronounced. "I'm only fifteen."

Her voice sounded small and scared.

"Oh, Christ," came a voice from just behind Haley, an edge of irritation in it. "Give the kid a break. Can't you see you're upsetting her? Take no for a fucking answer."

That was Kelsey Robbins.

The petite young woman was a fireball in human form, a foul-mouthed, no-nonsense bundle of raw energy who, in her own words, was fueled by rage and caffeine in epic quantities. This wasn't the first time she'd clashed with Haley since becoming acquainted with her.

Kelsey was here with Dave Shepherd, her far more mellow and perpetually stoned boyfriend. They were close friends of Bob Abernathy, who Haley was dating. Abrasive Kelsey, who otherwise seemed to harbor real affection for Bob, was always calling him "Fat" Bob. None of her friends, Bob included, ever admonished her for it, nor did the repeated insensitivity ever seem to bother any of them. What really puzzled Penny about this was not the lack of offense taken by Bob, who was a good-natured, easygoing guy.

But he was also not fat.

Like, at all. So ...

Haley glared at Kelsey. "Mind your business."

From her tone, it was clear she'd left an additional word unuttered at the end of that sentence.

Bitch.

Kelsey's scowling expression indicated a keen awareness of the silent epithet. She looked like she was on the verge of responding in some typically incendiary way when Bob intervened by plucking the bottle from Penny's trembling fingers and guzzling down a third of its remaining contents in one long pull.

"No use in wasting perfectly good liquor on a kid," he said, bringing the bottle away from his lips and passing it back to his pal Dave before Haley could reclaim it. "Ain't that right, Dave-o-rama?"

"Amen, brother," Dave said, proving he understood the implied assignment by immediately chugging down another sizable portion of the booze. He wiped his mouth with the back of a hand and made an exaggerated sound of appreciation. "Man, that hits the spot. I've been dying to get my drink on all day."

A smirking Kelsey snatched the bottle from her boyfriend and quickly downed what was left, tossing it over her shoulder as soon as it was empty. About a second later, it shattered on the cracked and faded asphalt of the dead shopping center's parking lot to sounds of dismay from other patrons farther back in the line.

Kelsey pumped a fist and made a whooping sound like a drunken sorority sister at a Saturday night mixer. "*Woo! Par-tay!*"

Penny put a hand over her mouth to cover a smile. Judging from her sister's look of seething annoyance, showing her amusement seemed inadvisable. The ironic thing was how the trio's spontaneous act of coordinated defiance had done worlds more to make drinking seem fun and appealing than any of her sister's hard-sell bullying tactics. Not enough to make her want to actually indulge, but it did make it possible to imagine some future version of herself enjoying drinks with friends. Maybe when she was in college or even a little later on.

Or maybe she'd be a teetotaler her whole life, who knew?

That was the thing about being fifteen.

Her future was a book filled with a lot of blank pages, and it'd be up to her to write her story any way she saw fit.

Haley stayed pissed off as the line ahead of them continued to shrink, the ticket booth drawing ever-nearer as patrons purchased their tickets and entered the carnival grounds through the adjacent turnstile. Her face was red and her eyes were wide circles radiating livid fury. She was biting down on her twitching bottom lip in an effort not to blow up at all of them. What sucked most about the way she was acting was how the worst of her scorn was reserved for Penny, which was evident every time her bulging eyes flicked toward her. There was what looked like real hatred in that expression.

Seeing it made Penny sad, almost made her cry.

She tried to imagine what it would be like to have an older sister who was capable of empathy, who actually loved and supported her, and had to turn away lest the tears actually start falling. Being vulnerable in that way would just earn her more of Haley's scathing derision, a perception heightened when she heard her sister mutter something mean that was clearly directed at her.

Stupid loser bitch.

Penny was sure this was a prelude to the explosion she'd been holding back, but then Bob leaned close to whisper something apparently soothing into Haley's ear. His voice was low enough that Penny was unable to make out a single word of what he was saying, but he continued speaking low in that same calm tone for nearly a full minute, only stopping when something he'd said prompted a giggle.

There was no mockery in this sound, just pure, happy amusement. The relief Penny felt at hearing it brought her the courage to risk looking Haley in the eye again. What she saw in Haley's expression wasn't exactly a renewal of empathy or regret for her behavior—that would've been too much to hope for—but there was also no return of her former harshness.

Penny was no fool, though.

She sensed the antipathy still lurking behind the happier façade. This was a respite from the rancor, nothing more. It made her wonder what her life could be like if Haley stayed with Bob Abernathy forever, maybe even got married and started a family of her own.

But, no, that would never happen. It wasn't Haley's style.

And she wouldn't wish a lifetime spent dealing with her sister's toxic personality on someone as kindhearted as Bob.

Just four people were still ahead of them in line. Two couples. Soon their own group would be at the booth, and shortly thereafter they'd pass through the turnstile and be inside the carnival. Penny couldn't wait. She'd still rather be just about anywhere else, but since that currently wasn't an option, she figured she'd make the best of the situation. The moment she passed through that turnstile, she would separate from the rest of their group and disappear into the crowd. Haley might be pissed at first, but Penny had a hunch what she'd mostly feel was relief.

The last couple ahead of them bought their tickets and went inside.

Barely more than a minute later, they had their own tickets in hand.

The instant she was through the turnstile, Penny executed her escape plan, zipping off into the crowd without warning. To her surprise, Haley did not immediately start shouting at her to come back. Her sister didn't say anything at all, in fact, a development that stirred an uneasy mixture of relief and disappointment in Penny.

She did her best to put all that out of her mind as she continued to thread her way through the crowd, but it was harder than she thought. The idea that her only sibling viewed her with such scorn and cared so little for her in general hurt just like it always did. She didn't have a lot of friends—not good close ones—and it would have been nice to have someone at home who had her back. But by now it was clear she would forever have no one she could depend on but herself.

More tears welled in her eyes at the thought, but she furiously wiped them away as anger began to bubble up beneath the surface of her sorrow. Not having anyone to depend on meant she had to become stronger, more mentally tough, because that was the only way she was getting through these last couple years of high school without losing her mind.

As her tears dried, she forced herself to slow down and get her breathing under control. She'd been moving at a pace shy of a sprint, which had required jostling her way through the surprisingly large crowd. More than once she'd been told to watch where she was going after bumping into someone. Several harsh epithets were hurled her way. One person had even given her a hard shove in the back. It was time to calm down before something even worse happened.

Moving at a slower walking pace allowed Penny to emerge from the tunnel vision that had consumed her and become more fully aware of her surroundings. The carnival's midway was lined on both sides with various attractions of the expected sort. She passed by ring toss and shooting gallery booths, lingered for a moment in the vicinity of a claw machine to observe as a middle-aged guy clumsily attempted to operate it. He was being loudly encouraged by a much younger woman Penny assumed was his daughter until she slipped a hand in his rear pocket and squeezed his ass.

As she moved on, she heard the loud *clank-clank-clank* of the Ferris wheel beginning to spin. She could see its illuminated rim revolving over on the other side of the midway, above the level of the booths and tents, the lights bright and colorful in the darkening sky.

Kids ran hither and thither through the crowd, laughing and squealing as they chased each other with plastic squirt guns. The old-timey organ sounds of carousel music filled the air from somewhere nearby, bouncy and charming at first, before briefly slowing in a weird way that was almost creepy. It was like listening to something played in a malfunctioning cassette player, the music still audible as the tape snagged and stretched. Hearing that happen made Penny's head hurt for a moment, but then the music resumed its previous bouncy tempo and the ache went away.

Weird.

A bunch of food vending booths and machines were spread throughout the midway. The sweet smells of funnel cakes, cotton candy, and fresh popcorn twitched her nostrils and stirred a slight rumble in her stomach. She hadn't previously felt hungry, but the smells were driving her crazy. Deciding that one of those funnel cakes would hit the spot, she dug out some cash and took a step in the direction of the stand where they were being sold.

Then she froze in her tracks, her attention snagged by something glimpsed in her peripheral vision. For another fraction of a second, a flashing instantly gone so fast it was possible to believe she'd only imagined it, there came a recurrence of the same mild ache she'd experienced upon hearing the slowed-down organ music.

Penny turned around and felt her breath catch in her throat.

She was standing in the center of the midway lane, with people continuing to stream in opposite directions in front of her, their forms almost blurry, like figures glimpsed through mist. What was strange about that was how clearly she could see the midway attraction on the other side of those scurrying forms, as if they were visions of separate worlds layered over each other. It was surreal and unsettling, and for a moment, she stood poised on the brink of bolting in the opposite direction, back toward the exit. Then that swimmy, unreal feeling passed, and the world felt fully in focus again, without the slightest sense of anything otherworldly in the air.

Penny shrugged.

Maybe it'd just been stress, the residual effects of intense anger leaving her body as her mood improved.

In front of her was a large red tent with a sign above the opening that read *Hall of Horrors*.

Before even realizing what she was doing, Penny was handing the cash originally earmarked for the purchase of a funnel cake over to a tall, lanky man in clown makeup. He was wearing red suspenders and colorful striped trousers. An old-fashioned sailor's hat was perched atop his frizzy head of red hair.

The grinning clown-man tore off a ticket for her and stepped aside to wave Penny into the tent. Pushing back a last shiver of trepidation, she moved through the opening and was swallowed by the darkness of the *Hall of Horrors*.

To read the rest of this story
please visit Bryan Smith's Patreon:
patreon.com/TheHorrorofBryanSmith

Two-time Splatterpunk Award winner Bryan Smith is the author of numerous novels and novellas, including *Depraved, 68 Kill, Slowly We Rot, The Killing Kind, House of Blood,* and *The Freakshow.* He is also the co-author of *Suburban Gothic,* written with Brian Keene. A new novel entitled *Monstrous* is forthcoming from Flame Tree Press in 2026. An acclaimed film version of 68 Kill was released in 2017. He'll have a story in the forthcoming Simon & Schuster anthology *The End of the World As We Know It: Tales of Stephen King's The Stand.* He lives in TN with his dog Mac and has an enduring affinity for strong, bitter beer and loud rock music of an increasingly ancient vintage.

<u>Social media:</u>
bryansmith.bsky.social

<u>Journal and exclusive fiction:</u>
patreon.com/TheHorrorofBryanSmith

<u>Signed books:</u>
bryansmithhorror.bigcartel.com

Other Grindhouse Press Titles

#666__*Satanic Summer* by Andersen Prunty
#111__*Drive-Thru of the Dead: Drayton Falls, Volume 1* by Bryan Smith
#110__*Inhospitable* by Ali Seay
#109__*Violência* by Sultan Z. White
#108__*From the Void* by Bryan Smith
#107__*Corpse Mountain* by Andersen Prunty
#106__*Depraved Halloween* by Bryan Smith
#105__*Dread Ink* by Bryan Smith
#104__*Jack and Mr. Grin* by Andersen Prunty
#103__*What Ever Happened to Jo Rose?* by Chris DiLeo
#102__*I Think I'm Alone Now* by Ali Seay
#101__*Cute Aggression* by Emily Lynn
#100__*Headless* by Scott Cole
#099__*The Killing Kind* by Bryan Smith
#098__*An Affinity for Formaldehyde* by Chloe Spencer
#097__*Kill The Hunter* by Bryan Smith
#096__*The Gauntlet* by Bryan Smith
#095__*Bad Movie Night* by Patrick Lacey
#094__*Hysteria: Lolly & Lady Vanity* by Ali Seay
#093__*The Prettiest Girl in the Grave* by Kristopher Triana
#092__*Dead End House* by Bryan Smith
#091__*Graffiti Tombs* by Matt Serafini
#090__*The Hands of Onan* by Chris DiLeo
#089__*Burning Down the Night* by Bryan Smith
#088__*Kill Hill Carnage* by Tim Meyer
#087__*Meat Photo* by C.V. Hunt and Andersen Prunty
#086__*Dreaditation* by Andersen Prunty
#085__*The Unseen II* by Bryan Smith
#084__*Waif* by Samantha Kolesnik
#083__*Racing with the Devil* by Bryan Smith
#082__*Bodies Wrapped in Plastic and Other Items of Interest* by Andersen Prunty
#081__*The Next Time You See Me I'll Probably Be Dead* by C.V. Hunt
#080__*The Unseen* by Bryan Smith
#079__*The Late Night Horror Show* by Bryan Smith